GOOD WOMEN

D1114510

GOOD WOMEN

HALLE HILL

HUB CITY PRESS
SPARTANBURG, SC

Cover Artwork © Simone Martin-Newberry
Hub City Editor: Katherine Webb-Hehn
Book Design Lead: Meg Reid
Proofreaders: Corinne Segal, Ko Bragg

Library of Congress Cataloging-in-Publication Data
Hill, Halle, 1994- author.
Good women / Halle Hill.
Description: Spartanburg, SC : Hub City Press, [2023]
Identifiers:
    LCCN 2023002453
    ISBN 9798885740173 (trade paperback)
    ISBN 9798885740180 (epub)
Subjects:
    LCSH: African American women—Fiction.
    Southern States—Fiction. Life change events—Fiction.
    LCGFT: Short stories.
Classification:
LCC PS3608.I4294 G66 2023
DDC 813/.6—dc23/eng/2023032
LC record available at https://lccn.loc.gov/2023002453

"Bitch Baby" originally apeared in *the Oxford American*; "The Truth About Gators" originally published in *New Limestone Review*; "Her Last Time in Dothan" originally published in *Joyland*; "Hungry" originally published in *The Southwest Review*.

Manufactured in the United States of America
First Edition

HUB CITY PRESS
200 Ezell Street
Spartanburg, SC 29306
864.577.9349 | www.hubcity.org

For Nedra and Lillian and Luvella and Elizabeth

i beg my bones to be good but
they keep clicking music and
i spin in the center of myself
a foolish frightful woman
moving my skin against the wind and
tap dancing for my life.

LUCILLE CLIFTON, "THE POET"

CONTENTS

SEEKING ARRANGEMENTS

We take the Greyhound down there, and Ron buys us the whole row, three people deep, so we can spread out. When we board the bus, I'm nervous to hand my ticket to the driver. I worry she somehow knows. I worry she judges me for letting this white man pay my bills, but she doesn't even notice us. Her badge reads HELLO MY NAME IS LAKEISHA! and she stamps our tickets with her eyes forward and her earbuds in, popping a wad of gum.

I choose the window seat. My toenails glisten in Cha-Ching Cherry red polish and my feet are spread across his lap. Now this is luxury! He pats the top of my brown feet and his hands shake like someone with Parkinson's. But he's fine, sort of, no Parkinson's—he's just hopped up on prednisone. In our seats, we go over the Boca action plan again, *if this then that*, and soon after, Ron falls asleep. LaKeisha's voice booms through the cabin while she tells us about Greyhound's policies, including the stops-per-miles rule. We only get four this trip. She takes her seat, puts her headphones back in, and starts driving; the bus moves faster than I imagined. Ron has his mouth open like fish. His palm is looped over my shin, holding me down. He turns fifty-one tomorrow, but he looks fifteen years older than that. While his chin hangs, I look at his face, I mean really look at it. His pores are large and he has red moles around the bulb of his nose. I count strips of light that line the aisle. It's a long way from where I am to the door. It's 10 a.m. I feel my stomach drop.

We were up talking for months every night on the phone before Ron brought me to see his mother in Florida. She lives in a Presbyterian retirement community with gates that keep people like me out. I met him on a dating site for wealthy men and twenty-something women. Me—a college dropout, broke, sleeping on an air mattress at my sister Sheena's house, helping with her girls—and him: 5'4", "set" with funds, too friendly, attentive, online doing nothing but talking to needy women like me. He hangs up the phone by saying, "Goodnight babe!" He calls me his "mutt" and "little hot thing." He says he's only teasing. He likes to chat on Yahoo! email. He thinks I'd look good with a shaved head.

Ron tells me I have a lot of potential but I talk too much. I'll be twenty-eight this fall, so my window is closing for a real career. The best way for me to get it going is to listen to him more. Ron's expertise spans over twenty years in the media industry, he likes to tell me. He made his millions after he sold his start-up business in the early 2000s. *"I created Myspace before Myspace!"* I can't find proof of this when I Google him though. He says he's seen all the gorgeous women in his day and I could be one of them if I really wanted to. So, with his help, I am trying.

We can't fly because Ron is sick. His blood is strong but his heart is weak. He has a pacemaker, an older model not built for airplane pressure. He's barely able to walk long distances, his face is swollen, and his neck is wide. When we met in person two weeks ago at The Cheesecake Factory in Green Hills, he looked nothing like he did online. I drove over from Lebanon in Sheena's Grand Prix. He kept coughing up phlegm into a seersucker handkerchief. He rented us a room at a Days Inn and tried to pay in cash. When we lay together that night, chest to chest, I called him my *big boy* while I ran my hands along his gummy pecs looking for the place he was cut into. But his chest looked smooth, even, and hairless.

On the bus, I keep his medicine bag with me at all times. I know what to do if he has a flare-up. I have his EpiPen, his steroids, and his inhaler. I keep the Benadryl, aspirin, and Zoloft. I have Band-Aids, and Tums, and teeny bottles of Pedialyte. I have turmeric capsules, and generic Cialis, and puffy white pills of Ambien. Whatever he needs, I have. I got him. But I don't know why he requires all this. And I don't know why I'm here. And I don't know exactly what's ailing him.

The window feels nice and cool against my back. The ride from Nashville to Florida is twenty-two hours in total, and we are almost halfway there. We have a stop in El Dorado soon, which I need because my foot is asleep, I have to pee, and I could use the fresh air. A man with big eyes sits behind us and talks to himself, loudly. He smells like vinegar, but I don't want him to be embarrassed that he stinks, so I turn my face toward the glass. Outside the window, a scythe moon sits above towering sweet corn fields. They go on and on, touching the indigo sky and I want to stretch my leg out further, but Ron is now in REM sleep, and I don't want to wake him. His breathing is shallow: *rise fall rise fall rise fall*. His breath catches and holds longer than normal and I sit up, alert, just in case. I think of stuffing the travel doughnut pillow over this entire face. I put a finger over his nose to check. Eventually he gulps the air.

I pull up the photo album on my phone with all the pretend party ideas I have for him: a Pinterest board filled with balloons and party hats and streamers. I wish I could buy him a big cake covered in pink fondant. *Happy Birthday, Ron!!* I want a Hallmark moment with him while I watch him eat big spoonfuls of cake without any worry of IBS. In my imagination, I'm planning something grand for him in Boca. But I just don't have the money. I scroll on my phone and I have six notifications, all of them from Sheena.

Where are you?

Where are you??

Hello??

Are you okay?

I'm sick of this shit Krystal.

No. really. Just let me know you're okay...please.

She's angry but I have to take this time for me. She knows I always come back, and I need to have boundaries. That's another thing he's helping me with. Boundaries. I am getting better at naming my needs. Ron says I'm getting better with standing up for myself. I'll be late on the rent this month again, but Sheena will understand. Ron says he'll pay me on the way back from Boca. And besides, Sheena's got me like that. I've only been gone a few days.

We cross over into Warner Robins city limits, and the man behind me with the big eyes starts acting crazy, rocking in his seat, muttering slurs. He gets louder and louder and he starts to smell worse. He's pissed himself. The man with the big eyes runs up to the front of the bus and starts yelling at LaKeisha.

"Let me off. Let me off now!"

When he grabs the back of her neck, I panic. The whole cabin is frozen, and a few passengers gasp. A Latina lady in the row next to me prays softly, and I watch her pull her two babies closer. LaKeisha jerks the bus over to the side of the road and opens the doors. It's pitch black and we're still in the middle of a corn field. The doors swing open into the hot June air, and the man with the big eyes bolts down the steps and runs with all his might into the corn. He runs and runs and runs until we don't see him anymore. Until he's just a blip. My heart beats out of my chest. After ten minutes or so, LaKeisha drives on and Ron wakes up. His drool is dry on his cheek.

"Miss anything, angel?"

I shake my head and look back out the window. The black sky makes my temples ache from the squinting. I keep looking for the man with the big eyes, but he doesn't show up.

It's 11p.m. when we make it to El Dorado. The layover here is around two hours, so we get off the bus in the Walmart parking lot and walk across the street to an Applebee's. I'm watching my figure at the moment, so Ron suggests we eat here so we can both have something. He's one of those men who will order for us and says things like, *A steak for me and perhaps a salad for the lady?* A waitress with a jet-black, box-dye rope braid down her back takes our order. Her breasts are cartoonish. Ron's eyes dart back and forth across her creped, sun-blotched cleavage.

The seats in the restaurant booth are cracked. Ron orders a Michelob Ultra and nurses it, and I have a few Long Island Iced Teas, top shelf, 'cause he spoils me like that. He says it's okay for me to loosen up every once in a while, and I can trust him to look after me. I have about four drinks and a Cobb salad with warm bacon bits.

Ron barely eats. He briefs me on what to do when we get to Boca. With his mother's dementia worsening, she doesn't remember much, and he wants her to think he's settled down with someone good. If she asks who I am, I say his fiancée. If she asks how we met, I say at work. If she asks when the wedding is, I say next summer. Ron reaches across the table to hold my hand. He takes it in his palm and rubs my knuckles, smiling warmly. I smile back and feel like I'm choking.

I realize how full my bladder is and run to the bathroom with double vision. It's hard to get my jeans unbuttoned, so I wet my pants a little as I plop on the toilet and scroll on my phone. Sheena sent me more texts, a picture of my nieces swinging at the park.

They miss you.

I lock my phone, wipe, and stumble back to the booth. I don't flush. I don't wash my hands. I don't look at myself.

When we get up to leave, my head starts to slosh and I reach for my bag to make sure I got him. Ron flips through his phone while I claw. I have it. I have the Naproxen, and the Allegra, and the Centrum One A Day Men's Health Formula vitamins. He helps walk me back to the bus, but I still know I have anything he could need if he asks for it. Everything is closing but neon lights from the Cheetah strip club blink in the distance. Ron takes me by my arm and pulls me up the stairs onto the bus. I say *hey* to LaKeisha but she ignores me.

The El Dorado newspaper has a "Ms. Goldie Girl's Horoscope" column where you can read a weekly forecast for your zodiac sign. I ripped one from the rack before I re-boarded. I pull out my copy and read Ron his. When I have this many drinks, I talk to him way too close to his face. I drop the Ambien into his palm and read aloud about Geminis. It says something about the moon being in perfect transit for his love and creativity. And how he is on the cusp of a rebirth.

I take the horoscope as a sign that I'm in the right place at the right time with the right man. I'm yapping about his astrological traits (great with communication, difficulty in expressing emotion!) when Ron puts his hot mouth on mine. I hate it but don't push it off. It's wet as he pulls me closer with the stronger of his arms. This time they aren't shaking. The Ambien makes him handsy but I've been drinking too, so it's no one's fault. We sloppy-kiss until he starts slurring his words. As he drifts, his mouth slides off me and he slumps in the seat. I see a gash on his translucent hand, probably where he scratched himself. I dig through my bag and find a Band-Aid and some Neosporin. I dab the wound with a cotton swab. It has a gloss from the salve that shines.

But I fix him up just fine. I look after him. The cabin lights cut out, and I'm so gone I can't focus on his face anymore. I look up to the front of the bus, at the back of LaKeisha's neck. She rubs the spot in a circle where the man with the big eyes grabbed her. For a moment, I think this is it. Right now, I can decide it's over. I'll bring LaKeisha, too.

She and I should make a run for it. She could park this piece of shit and we'll bolt. Arm in arm. We could find our way.

I know I could get off right here if I wanted to. ✹

HONEST WORK

Days this bad belonged to Maudette. She felt the sorrow drop then pick back up, same as always, as she verged right toward the Cherry Street exit, gunning for Chilhowee Park. It was a quarter to 7 a.m. as she pulled into the fairgrounds lot for her Thursday 6:30-a.m.-on-the-dot shift. In the parking lot she flipped down the driver's seat mirror, pinched her cheeks, and rubbed Vaseline on her chapped lips. Eighteen and already miserable. This was when she thought of her mother, Sylvia, and the men. And it was this thought that filled her blue.

As Maudette made her way to her manager's kiosk to receive her assignments for the day, she tried not to think of the violet marks on her mother's wrists. Her boss, Donnie, sat in his black pleather chair and rocked like a toddler, watching you-are-not-the-father reruns on his hand-crank TV. A space heater sat at his ankles, though it was the dead of summer.

"Right on time," he griped as he handed her a playing card–sized paper printout of her schedule. She slid the sheet into a green lanyard around her neck. Ham from Donnie's Egg McMuffin stained the edge of the paper. For a moment Maudette considered eating it.

She looked down at her placements. It wasn't a great day:

7-11: Entrance Gate

11-1: Terry the Snapping Turtle Mascot—
Performance & Mingling

1-2: Lunch (Worker Break 15 min) & Service (45 min)

2-4: Corny Cornpone Food Hut

4-7: Tilt-A-Whirl

Maudette stood in her work Crocs at the center of the world: WELCOME TO THE MILLER VALLEY FAIR. At the gate, she mouth-breathed to avoid whiffs of hot peanut oil and earthy barn animals.

It sure looked pretty, though, in the Valley. From the entrance, you got one of the finest views of East Tennessee. The morning sky, inflamed with metallic whoring. The blue ribbon livestock, skyscrapers of dried tobacco, God's eye and eight-pointed star quilts.

So far every night that week, the sun set and the high held steady at ninety-two degrees. By mid-morning, Maudette's lower back would be soaked from the dry heat coming off the pavement, the kind that stuck too close to the skin. Evening was the best, but she rarely got to work this booth at sunset.

Looking down the line, she noticed the end-of-week exhibitors setting up. Today, the foodstuffs categories were on display: East Tennessee native produce and sweet lattice pies almost too pretty to eat. Last Monday, Maudette stalled going home and instead wandered about the booths in search of the entomology display tucked in a back corner: beetles, cicadas, and moths with soft, fragile wingspans the length of her palm sat suspended in white shadow boxes. She admired the precise labor so closely, her nose fogged the glass. Each specimen knew its place and sat spaced equal centimeters apart. Nothing about her felt this delicate. Maudette watched the people waiting for their ranking and the coveted honor: a $100 Food City gift card. She wished she had something special to look forward to.

At the booth, the morning sun blazed. Back home, her mother would be taking her first client of the day.

The line grew. Maudette pinched the indentions off each tab, throwing the portions in the ADMIT bucket, soft-spoken *Welcomes* barely escaping over her teeth. She saw some familiar faces: a group of teachers from the county high school, the home-schooled children who protested outside the gates on Sunday, and some of the late night good-ole-boys who frequented the Taco Bell parking lot one block from her house, their trucks revving though the early mornings. Surrounded by a pack of squealing teenagers and wearing a three-piece suit, there was Deacon James. He'd driven forty minutes from Blue Pasture Baptist to reward his youth with a trip to the fairgrounds. They were there to celebrate handing out seventy-one gospel tracts downtown and making it through their seventy-two-hour Daniel fast. At the ticket kiosk, Deacon James looked down, never meeting Maudette's eyes.

Maudette knew Deacon James drove out this way often, going a few miles past the fairgrounds exit to see her mother Sylvia.

If Maudette was home, she'd open the door after four knocks and lead him down to the basement, where it smelled like incense and yeast, throbbing with instrumental Amy Grant. A regular, Deacon James came to the house twice a month. Maudette felt indifferent about her mother's money and could manage the men; they'd been there since she could remember, but there was something about Deacon's cash that felt distinctively dirty. Most of them were harmless, like eighty-two-year-old Clyde who, while waiting for his appointment on Tuesdays, watched *Wheel of Fortune* with Maudette at 7 p.m. on WVLT. But for Deacon, Maudette didn't think it was about pleasure. She heard the whimpers. It sounded like it was about power. It sounded like he enjoyed causing Sylvia unwanted physical pain. *We don't need him,* Maudette often thought.

Even with the music and the door closed, Maudette could hear the noises from upstairs. As men like Deacon released, she'd turn the TV up louder, the green bar of the volume reaching its maximum. The cash jar sat on the table behind her on a wall that held all her photos and diplomas—most recently, the one from the Sunshine Central Cosmetology Institute. She could now apply foil highlights, relax new growth, and do a roller set, but so could every other girl from Clinton to Maynardville. She had trouble finding a salon that would take her.

At his last visit, Deacon James stuffed 200 single-dollar bills, bank fresh, in the jar with his functional hand (the other was paralyzed, small like a child's, from a birth defect) and shuffled out the door. Maudette watched him leave, satisfied as he met the rest of his day with damp hair and a flushed face.

Sylvia said it was in the touch. The body knows the difference between sexual and medical and spiritual so she focused mostly on how she intended others to know her. It didn't matter what her clients felt or thought they felt; the intention of her body was pure. She made her money this way, through her touch work and energy healings, oiling bodies daily.

Sylvia had moved from Alabama to Tennessee when she was young. She'd studied business at the University of Tennessee, and in her junior year she had started sleeping with her teacher's assistant, Ryan, an ABD adjunct from Chapel Hill. They got married in Sylvia's last year of school, and soon after, Sylvia got pregnant with a baby she named for her grandmother, Maudette. She was happy until Ryan started working late, smelling different, and messing up—saying other women's names during sex. Maudette was only two years old.

JUSTINE LOVE: LIGHT-PRACTITIONER
INVISIBLE MEDICINE + MASSAGE THERAPY!

The banner caught Sylvia's eye during a routine trip to Kohl's. She'd been on her own, raising Maudette, for a few years. A pretty brown woman with translucent hazel eyes stood at her pop-up at East Towne Mall. With a pin-straight back and pit bull–like focus, the woman watched the passing people, smelling for the right somebody. Sylvia looked at her hands, full of returns and frumpy clothes for her couch-potato life, and felt insecure. Tall and long-legged, with wide-set eyes, and a small gap between her front teeth, Ryan called her *exotic* in the old days. But at that moment, she felt dully plain. She swore her brown jowls were getting loose, her skin splotched with sunspots, and she now had deep frown lines. She passed the booth a few times, wanting to seem skeptical. While shy, and smart enough to know better, Sylvia was a sucker for get-rich-quick-schemes. Three years ago it was Young Living, a few months ago Arbonne, and one week earlier she'd given up on Mary Kay. Maybe this was the sign she'd been waiting for.

Justine shone like a Barbie out of the box. Her skin glowed bright with Botox tightness, pulling thin at the edges of her hair, slicked with pomade. With a wide grin, Sylvia saw the back left of Justine's mouth was missing most of her molars, but she smiled anyway.

The banners promoted a lot of things: working from home, stable income, financial independence. Right outside the automatic doors of Kohl's, Justine stood, almost blocking people's way in, describing her business with words that were new to Sylvia, ones that she had never heard of before like *reiki* and *chakra*. So, Sylvia stopped and talked with Justine, and Justine took one look at her, felt her energy, and told her she was a *natural*. Right there, Sylvia signed up and bought some of her supplements, DVD workshops, and installment packages. Because Justine told her she had to make an investment before she could make the money back, Sylvia paid $300 in cash, savings she had put away for a new A/C window unit. She figured she could crack a window and make it a bit longer in the heat.

A few days later, Sylvia began the *assessments*: the call sessions, sound baths, biofeedback and inner healing visioning. Soon, she became an apprentice, then a partner, watching Justine do her sessions on people and work out their traumas.

A lot of the people they helped were the elderly or lonely, people who needed touch. But there were also the men who needed help surrendering. Justine told Sylvia sometimes some men needed something extra than the others. Sylvia caught on quickly, quietly thrilled with being wanted on her terms.

In her years of doing the work, there were never any other clients. Only the men.

Maudette liked to take the long way home after work, but the drive was never long enough. Most evenings she walked in with her head held down, wiping away the crumbs from her gas-station powdered doughnuts. Her raggedy khaki Old Navy shorts rode up between her thighs, which made her tug at her crotch every five minutes.

Lately, Maudette came home to her mother in long-sleeved blouses and lit Nag champa on the altar while Sylvia sipped on her healing elixir of kombucha, which was mostly gin. Her mother had managed to make a decent life for her and Maudette as a light practitioner. They paid rent, took an annual vacation to Pigeon Forge, but something always lingered. The Nag champa never rid the home of the stench of hot bodies.

Last night, Sylvia had looked at Maudette up and down, slowly, sipping her drink and drizzling tahini on their spinach salad as Maudette took her place at the table. Maudette poked at the Bob Evans TV dinner using her fork to jab the soggy macaroni noodles and sloshed down the yellow slop with a tall glass of Big K Orange

Soda. After finishing the tin, her mother looked at her with proud pity. Maudette could feel a lecture coming, how her mother felt good she could put food on the table, how the cash jar was stuffed to the brim. Something about three clients that day. She was right.

"We have so much abundance, Maudette. Look around you."

Abundance? Maudette scanned the room—she saw their broken-down couch, their big back TV, the hole in the ceiling they never got around to fixing.

Sylvia held a large Blue Lace Agate to her forehead and smiled. With her other hand, she dangled a clear pendulum over Maudette's head and nodded. "Your sacral center is off, dear. Try wearing more orange."

Maudette grabbed her mother's wrist to stop her. Sylvia winced. Maudette had tried asking about the bruises before, but it was the one conversation that was off limits. Last time she mentioned it, Sylvia hurled her tincture glass against the kitchen linoleum and collapsed into rageful tears.

"May I be excused, please?" Maudette asked. She stood up slowly, tugging at the corners on her shirt.

For months, Maudette hoped to get a good enough job so her mom could rest and just *be*, but so far, no luck. Her state fair pennies surely weren't cutting it.

Later that evening, while Sylvia watched an old episode of *Bonanza*, Maudette sat next to her on the couch and reached for her mother's hand. She moved her thumb gently across the blue splotches on Sylvia's wrist. Sylvia kept her eyes on the TV and snatched her hand back.

As Maudette stood to leave, Sylvia stuck her chin out to the ceiling for her daughter to kiss. Maudette leaned next to her mother and pecked her chin with curled lips. Sylvia squeezed Maudette's face and looked in her eyes and passed her a wad of cash.

"I love you, Maudette. Please don't forget it."

A toddler at the Baby Cicada interactive station shit all over the floor. Maudette had to clean it all herself. On her hands and knees with a gallon of bleach, she scrubbed and scrubbed and scrubbed in the hot sun but the shit wouldn't come out.

While doing a performance as Terry the Snapping Turtle, she missed her cue and panicked to keep up with the beat. An anxious misstep caused her claw to get caught in the AV cords. Her ankle looped in the rubber when she went to pivot then sashay. She fell to the ground and her audience of six gasped.

At lunch, she huffed down her usual: fried Oreos, a corn dog combo, and Mountain Dew. She stuffed some fries in her pockets for later, then made her way to the Food Hut where, in a hair net, she served turkey legs and chitlins in plastic, Davy Crocket–themed bowls.

"DAMN. Something smells like dookie in here!" her co-worker Michelle screamed from the register.

Maudette quietly sniffed her collar hoping it wasn't her.

It was.

It happened when Maudette was born. The moment Sylvia pushed her out, she felt something burst in her chest, her body felt cold in an instant, as if she dipped underwater. Her ob-gyn said arrhythmia was common after vaginal births, but Sylvia swore it was Maudette. Her daughter was making her presence known.

"I always felt you'd be a sad little girl, Maudy," she'd tell her.

When it was time for her final shift of the day, Maudette felt warm in her heart. It wasn't much but the Tilt-A-Whirl was *her* place. The final shift was *her* time.

From the control panel, she had a full view of the sun setting in the valley. She could see a sliver of river too; she loved to watch blue herons glide over the water, their long bodies spreading over the surface, grazing almost close enough to skim. The sun dipped down into the water and the sky was melting in orange and purple. Soft pink ripples of clouds sewed through the expanse. Maudette sighed and settled into her Crocs, relaxing for the first time that day.

But when she saw the crowd from Blue Pasture approach, her head began to ache. Deacon James stood right at the front and smiled while he watched the lights of the ride shimmer.

The young saints stood in line, their bodies buzzing while they brushed up against one another. They held their sixty-two ounce Slurpees in their hands, and they smiled wide—red dye 40 staining the tartar around their plump, pink gum lines. They shoved funnel cakes down their mouths and shoved each other, bracing for fifteen turns high in the air. Maudette readied herself in anticipation, sweat pricked in her armpits.

As the youth group belched at one another, Maudette squared her shoulders in authority, whisper-barking protocol. They weren't listening. They were lost in joy as they lined up to load themselves into the cars. They begged Deacon James to get on and ride with them: *Deacon! Deacon! Deacon!*

The Miller Valley Fair had a strict-ish policy at the Tilt-A-Whirl: only three allowed, maximum four if you were really pushing it. Maudette undid the latch at the entrance and stood, trying one more time to get their attention.

"Listen please! After I open the gate, no more than three inside the car. Oh, and place your ticket in the ADMIT bu…"

A swarm of teens ran into the ride and buckled themselves in. Rocking on the edges of the ride, they pretended the cars were dinghys caught in a rough current. They bucked back and forth. At the car furthest to the left, Maudette noticed four people squished in three seats, the extra spot taken by Deacon James. He was in a seat Maudette needed to monitor, as the belt was weakening at the hinges and would come undone with anyone who put too much of their body weight on the latch.

The youth group clapped for the Deacon, chanting—"Twirl! Twirl!"—for Maudette to start the ride.

Deacon James grinned at Maudette. "Well, you heard them."

She felt heat rise on the inside and chewed like a rat on the skin in her cheeks. One girl snatched a Slurpee out of a boy's hand and held the straw in-between her index and thumb, sucking slowly. She turned to the control panel and rolled her eyes.

"When is this thing gonna start?"

The whole ride erupted in laughter. Deacon James held his hand up in protest. The girl sat up, kept sucking and kept looking, then turned, tossing her hair over her shoulder. They grew more and more impatient. Maudette's chest started to burn.

It was always turn number six that did the inevitable. Maudette didn't know if it was better to warn people about it or not. The combination of the fair food, hay dust, and frozen corn syrup made certain people queasy. In the summer when classes let out, young couples would come to the park in the evening and saunter. The boys would take their sweeties on the ferris wheel, then the teacups, then march up to the Tilt-A-Whirl, dip can indentions bearing through the back pockets of their Carhartts. Their lovers would *ooh* and *ah* as the blinding lights whirred around and around above them, floating in the big night sky. They'd hold hands and kiss. As they waited in the line they'd devour their treats, cinnamon-sugared lard falling down their chins and into their hoisted cleavage.

After getting strapped in, participants would be hoisted up in the air and spun fifteen times. The first turns brought joy. As more came so did the looks of terror. On turn four, the panic set in. Turn five was touchy—either a delirious, bubbling laugh or wet belching. For the chosen few, the dough and corn syrup caused a reaction, making them projectile vomit in the air until the ride came to a halt. Embarrassed, they were ready to bolt once they landed; they squirmed in discomfort. Maudette, in thin plastic gloves she swiped from the Food Hut, would unbuckle them and pass a paper towel to them if they needed it. She always felt sort of guilty. She saw the humiliation in their faces and tried to comfort them, but most people ran as soon as she let them out.

With a quick wipe down of a rag soaked in hot water and Simple Green, though, the ride was ready, and some-how, some way, people stepped up to the nonsense again. This was Maudette's life, Monday through Sunday, all summer long.

Maudette assumed her position toward the back of the control panel. She turned the key to start and the ride creaked to life. A breeze came off the machine and lights danced in circles off the metal. Muzak played in a warped, drowning key. The sun almost dissolved in the water now; only a hot orange sliver sat in half above the stillness. Maudette's mouth watered as she looked at the bucket of Simple Green, then back at Deacon James while he, she was certain, managed feelings of nausea. As the turns increased in speed, his face grew paler. He gripped at his seatbelt that was coming undone.

One twirl, two, three, four, five, and then there was sweet six. Like clockwork, the puke started to flow. From each car people leaned over the wayside, retching. It dripped down the wooden sides of the orbs like strawberry puree. Maudette kept her focus. Soon, Deacon James joined, too. As he tried to save face, he leaned over the side and lost his grip on the seatbelt. While the car turned again he flew like a rag doll to the other side. He began to shriek. Maudette hovered her hand over the stop button but kept her eyes on the Tilt-a-Whirl.

The ride continued to turn and it flung Deacon James again, again. The three riders from his youth group tried to grasp on to him but could not reach. His back slammed into the door of the ride. He moaned as his thigh wedged in the latch of the entrance door and began ripping at the flesh above his knee. Blood spilled onto the floor of the car, mixing with the sour pink creamy sludge.

"Someone save him!" a young father, desperately trying to cover his daughter's eyes, yelled from the line.

Maudette watched as people flocked to the Tilt-a-Whirl. Donnie was beside her now, placing his hands on her station. His face was bloodshot.

"Turn this thing off. Turn the FUCKING ride off!" he screamed in Maudette's face, his spit splashing across her flushed skin. Tears welled in Maudette's eyes as she swallowed a dry lump in her throat. Her legs locked. She looked at Donnie. She didn't move. Donnie pushed her out of the way and shut the ride down manually. The gears whined to a halt. Everything got still. The crowd had multiplied. It seemed like the whole park gathered right there in the midst of all that commotion. The sun was below the hills now.

Maudette took off. She grabbed her bags from behind the podium, knelt to secure the backs of her Crocs against her heels, and ran. She cut through the trees, ran past her car in the parking lot, then the entrance, all the way to the road. The sirens from the ambulance were getting closer. Maudette swatted mosquitoes from her face and kept running and running.

She stopped at a bus stop a mile or so away and checked her watch. It was after 8 p.m. and Sylvia was waiting for her, maybe tonight with Buddy's Bar-B-Q and Idahoan mashed potatoes. She would be there sitting at the table patiently, speech slurred from her elixir by now, and the bruises coming through the concealer under her eyes.

Sylvia waited for Maudette to get off work but felt unusually exhausted. She poured another glass of elixir and fluffed her hair in the mirror. She looked at herself in her work set, half amused, half in disbelief. She saw a galaxy bruise above her stomach, she pressed into it with two fingers. She couldn't believe where her body had taken her, she couldn't believe the people she'd met in her practice: once the mayor, once even the governor. But somehow she felt she'd let her girl down. She was nearing midlife, wanting her daughter's approval. "Isn't that something?" she said to herself. It was thirty minutes past 8 p.m. when Maudette typically got home. She was late. That wasn't like her.

Sylvia felt queasy. She paced, then poured another drink and sat back on the couch.

In times of crisis, Justine taught her a mantra to repeat: *I am divinely protected.*

Sylvia imagined her Maudette saying it over and over, and then she drifted asleep.

When the bus came, Maudette hopped on and took a seat toward the back. It was just her and the bus driver, an older Black man with a tired face. They didn't say anything to each other. Maudette looked out the window and shoved her hands in her pockets and fiddled with the dollars her mother gave her. She imagined ripping them to pieces. An ambulance went by, this one in a different direction off to someone she hadn't hurt. She watched it fly.

As the bus made its slow crawl toward her part of town, Maudette caught her breath but had no more tears. She picked at the rawness in between her thighs and felt better.

From the bus stop, Maudette walked through her neighborhood, the streets quiet and wide. From outside the front door she looked into the windows. In the living room, Sylvia sprawled on the sofa, sleeping deeply, in a cheap set of Warner's red and black lingerie.

Maudette put her keys in the front door and pushed gently, catching the screen door. Dragon's Blood incense burned on the coffee table. Maudette put a blanket on her mother and tucked the corners in around her arms and feet, took her palm, and smoothed her hair back. She thought about the two of them, somewhere in another world, where it wasn't so hard. Different women, a different life. But what use was imagining? Maudette sat on the floor, her back against the couch. Watching cars pass out the screen door, she took the money out of her pocket and thumbed through the bills.

She turned, watched her mother's breathing, and noticed the flesh around her chest, her heart pulsing out of the thin skin. Growing up, Maudette's favorite place was under her mother's chin, with her nose pressed to her neck, smelling her perfume while she sat ear to chest, listening to the out-of-beat rhythm.

Maudette remembered how her own chest burned, how fast she was running—the dew-wet night, the mildewed grass, the screaming cicadas making her ears go in and out. The fair lights were glowing like a thousand eyes above her. Watching. Knowing the only place she was ever headed was home. ✻

HER LAST TIME IN DOTHAN

Uncle Otis's heart is swelling like a balloon. It'll burst and he'll die soon, Mama says. Mama talks on the phone to Aunt Loretta about it on the way down to Dothan.

"I told him to lay off that coke, Roberta. I told him. I've been off it for months now, probably a year. He just don't listen, girl."

Mama keeps it on speakerphone because she likes two hands on the wheel even though she expects me not to listen. But in some ways, I think she wants me to hear.

I Googled it before we left, *Dothan*. In the Word, it's the place where Joseph's brothers dropped him in a well and sold him into slavery. In Alabama, it's the peanut capital of the world. Second to that fame was the cotton. I watch the white tufts out the window—they look soft enough to hold. Aunt Loretta gets to bullshitting: says Grandma is doing great, better than ever! Mama sucks her teeth in when she hears this.

It's been the two of us ever since Daddy got the job working in corporate at Weigel's. First Black man that high up. Ever since, we've been alone together, me and her. But that's okay. It's part of the sacrifice. We've got more than ever now, a big brick house in a cul-de-sac with a gas fireplace that comes on with the flick of a switch. I've got my own room with my own phone and my own shower. I changed schools this year, too. Now I wear a collared shirt and wool uniform. I perm my hair. I met somebody.

At every stoplight Mama mutters meditations her reiki master gave her. *I can release this, I am whole.* Again and again and again. She's got a life coach as well. He recommended she take a new approach to her fear around dementia. She's been taking this Buddhist class he recommended at the local library; it's about grief and non-attachment.

When we get to Dothan, we pick up Aunt Loretta and her half-brother, Uncle Otis, and take them to eat at Outback Steakhouse. All my other aunts call him "the bastard." They hate him and swear his mama took their daddy Melvin away, but Aunt Loretta kept a soft spot for him.

Aunt Loretta is Mama's cousin, but it's rude for me to call her by her first name, and Cousin Loretta sounds too country, so I call her Aunt. Same for Otis. And when I look at them in the rearview I can't help but think how opposite they are. Aunt Loretta is as skinny as a twig and as yellow as a piece of butter cake. And when Uncle Otis closes his eyes to blink, I'm certain if it was real dark at night, I couldn't find him even if I was looking.

We hoped to take Grandma with us to Outback, but Aunt Loretta says she's staying at her friend Janie's house for the evening. She scratches at herself, behind her elbow. I count four gold-plated shrimp-looking rings across her knuckles. She's wearing perfume, and it stinks, cheap White Diamonds.

"They wanted to watch *M*A*S*H*." She looks down when she says this.

I can tell Mama doesn't buy this, but we're hungry and it's been a long trip, so she doesn't press. In the booth, I focus on the appetizers. I shove pumpernickel bread gobbed with white butter in my mouth and feel around for my Tracfone in my back pocket. Mama wants to know everything new with Loretta and Otis, and Uncle Otis keeps grazing Loretta's hand when they reach for the Bloomin' Onion. Loretta doesn't swat his hand away, though, just scoots from him and says something about how she's so hungry she could gobble a horse. Mama and her catch eyes, before Loretta acts stumped by the menu again, taking her time as if she's really that curious, as if she wasn't a woman who knew exactly what she wanted to eat.

Loretta orders the Surf 'n' Turf cooked medium and a double Dark and Stormy. She eats it all, smacking down even the tails. Uncle Otis gets a T-bone, medium rare, and his skin looks just like it, gray and pockmarked. I hear the gristle tear while he cuts it. Both of them scarf down their food like they haven't eaten in days. They spoon in loaded mashed potatoes while chewing bites of broccoli drenched in A1. I'm getting nauseous. Loretta keeps commenting on the fancy foods, saying how broke she is with big, puppy eyes, even though she has a fresh roller set.

All the while, Uncle Otis nearly knocks his plate from the table, sawing that musty steak.

"You have to go against the grain." He grins.

The meat doesn't move. I grab a chip and try to load the max amount of spinach dip on, only to drop the glob beneath the table. I grunt, then poke around on my phone under the Formica. It lights up. Nothing.

Even in the dimmed restaurant fluorescents, Uncle Otis doesn't look good, and it's true: The cocaine is making his heart swell. He'll be dead three months from now and we won't go to the funeral. But at the Outback, he has Aunt Loretta and Mama and me laughing.

Otis rubs Loretta's knee in circles slowly a few times. He goes over the knee cap, like he's fluffing the skin there. Plumping it. I keep watching Loretta, hoping she'll say something, and my face turns hot. She smiles at Mama, full of quarter-colored caps, takes a sip, then moves his hand higher. The waitress brings the check and Mama takes out her thick American Express.

"Ohh, you something now, ain't you?" Loretta hoots.

"Girl, whatever."

"Well in that case, what do y'all got for dessert?" Uncle Otis almost splits in two. He stares at the middle of the credit card. The silver soldier on the front looks annoyed; he knows we don't got it.

"Whatever you want, you can have. Order the whole goddamn menu!" Mama drinks her Painkiller and shakes back the ice. She doesn't cuss like that at home because her life coach says it's crude: *A foul mouth robs a cheery heart, invokes the evil eye,* he reminds her.

"Thank you for tending to Mama. You know I wish I could." She grinds on her ice pellets for a minute. "I can't believe she's almost eighty-seven."

Otis looks Mama all over. Then he stares her in the eye and smiles. He has little dimples I didn't see before.

"You just never age, do you, Roberta? Looking as beautiful as ever."

"Ha. It's only concealer and fillers, don't let me fool you."

"No, it's that good heart of yours." He looks down her shirt. It's used Burberry she bought on eBay.

"You never forget us po' folk down here, huh?"

"Nigga, please." Mama looks at me and bugs her eyes out. I stuff more buttered bread and squeeze my knees together.

We end up ordering one of every dessert with coffees, and Uncle Otis belches the rest of the meal. He smells like a dumpster. I glare up at him but he doesn't notice because he's eating cheesecake.

It's late. The table is wet with drip from our drinks. Us women are ready to go, but he gets back to tearing up that old, raggedy piece of steak, looking down, saying softly, "Excuse me."

Me and Mama stay at the La Quinta in the center of town next to the Confederate bust of General Beauregard. Usually, we stay at a Hilton Garden Inn at least, but we don't want to seem high sadity. I like it though. The room is big! Two queen beds and lots of Neutrogena French milled soap I press to my nose and smell. I watch *CSI: Miami* on the bed while Mama looks for roaches and cameras. She doesn't find either, but there is mold in the back corner of the shower, so she calls down on the white phone to tell them about the spreading spores. They say if we don't say nothing about it on Facebook they'll give us the room for free so she ends up telling me to stand toward the front of the shower where the mold isn't when I wash up. Later, I keep the soap to my nose while I bathe, staring at the black slime.

I've been talking to Cory from my Algebra class on my Tracfone at night after Mama goes to sleep. On the last day of 7th grade we traded numbers but I haven't said anything to anyone about my grown folk's business. He tells me he can talk in the evenings after 9 when his minutes boot up. Last night I checked to see if Mama was asleep then I started texting him. But I stopped and pretended to be asleep when I heard some whimpering, it went on forever.

Before school let out, Heather told me Cory gave her his number, too. But I don't care. What we have is real.

Loretta lives on the corner of Poplar and Third. We go to her house the next day to pick up Grandma. She looks dead. And the house isn't nothing to look at, neither. It sags in the middle and the front porch is all but broke off. Overgrown Begonias crowd the front door. In the yard, I see two pit bulls chained up to an oak tree. The names "Beauty" and "Daisy" are embroidered in valentine pink on their collars.

When I hug Grandma, I'm afraid I'll snap her. She looks all of ninety-something pounds, her dentures poke out of her mouth, and she doesn't know who we are. Aunt Loretta is on food stamps and buys all her "sustenance" for Grandma off her WIC voucher. But she can't afford a lot, so Grandma is stuck eating Hungry Man XXL meat-loaves and Great Value meal replacement shakes. Aunt Loretta takes us inside and offers us some tap water. We both say no and I go to sit on the couch. *Judge Mathis* is on. Grandma sits across from us in her rocker. She stares off in space with her mouth open.

"Hey Ma," Mama says.

She reaches to hug her. As Mama holds her, Grandma pats her shoulders like a stranger, not a daughter. Her face looks frozen, stony, like someone who's had a lobotomy.

We've only been down to Dothan one other time, when we moved Grandma here from Chicago. She'd left Alabama long ago with some passing-through man she met somewhere at some bar. He left eventually. But she stayed there, started doing hair, had her daughters, made a little life, and got older. But then her memory started going. She left the gas stove on all day and got lost coming back from her walks around the block.

We shopped grandma around, looking for a caretaker. With our new life, the burden of her staying with us was not even an option, and we couldn't afford a retirement home. The only person we found was Aunt Loretta, who offered to take care of her in Dothan if Mama paid her rent.

To get to her, we flew from Tennessee to Illinois on United. I kept my ticket. From the plane, the world looked like dishwater. Brown blotches blurred beneath me. Stopping first at O'Hare, we drove over to Maywood, to the house she purchased for her girls and herself in her late forties: a tiny, narrow home with a cement basement, large porch, and kitchen with barred windows, which flooded with light.

On a Wednesday, we packed Grandma's belongings in a Mayflower truck outside her front door. As she slept, we went through her things, sorting them as essential or give-aways.

The movers drove the freight to Alabama, and we followed them a day later, flying out of Midway back south. We told Grandma how good it would be for her to go.

"You're going home!"

Home home home, we said to her, while she waited, mostly mute.

Crossing back into the sticky Dothan heat, even in winter, she looked deep in memory, as if she sensed the knowing of the place, smelling deep, closing her eyes, watching scenery repeat on reel out her window.

Mama says she's gonna take Grandma out for a few hours so I have to stay at Loretta's. "Gross," I whisper under my breath. It's kinda fun though once we get warmed up. She puts on some Earth, Wind, and Fire and pours me a glass of Moscato, my first ever. She says I can have some if I shut up about it. It tastes like sour Minute Maid.

She asks if I have a boyfriend while she lights a cigarette. I want to tell her about my man, but I'm too shy. We flip through a *Jet Magazine* and talk about hair styles. I tell her I want box braids all the way to my butt crack. She says she has a friend who could hook me up. We drink some more, and my head swims and I start giggling and swaying in the living room. Loretta comes with me.

We bump to the beat. I've got stars in my eyes.

"Girl, this makes me feel eighteen again!" she sings and twirls. "Like I am still wide eyed and fresh. Like I ain't never done a bad thing in my life."

It's a while later when I realize I've drifted off. The TV is still on, making the room light up. My phone says it's midnight, and Mama still isn't back. I have one missed call from her and a voicemail tells me she'll be home soon. I yawn and get up. I go to find the bathroom, wash out my eyes, and poke around Loretta's medicine cabinet (Lifestyle condoms, red enema, Mitchum deodorant), when I hear someone moan. I hear Loretta telling someone, "Go deeper." I hear someone else, a man, I think. Walking down the hallway, I get closer to the sounds, and I can't help it, something makes me look, and when I peek around the corner, blood drains from my face to my feet. I see that same pockmarked face from the Outback rolling around, pressed in Loretta's milky neck. I see a big body pushing in and out. I feel my knees buckle. My head rises above my body.

I walk with sea legs to the front porch and sit down on the concrete. Shaking, I try to find my bearings. Beauty and Daisy howl at me, jowls toward the sky.

In the morning, we take Grandma out for a good breakfast. At Waffle House she orders a pecan waffle and a hot coffee and the waitress who takes our order wears tiny butterfly clips that catch the light and flutter, and her eyeshadow is baby powder blue. It creases in the socket. Grandma calls her Madam Butterfly.

We have a sleepover. We take Grandma back to the La Quinta, where she plops on the bed and takes her t-shirt and bra off and her breasts droop everywhere, her nipples pointing down. She takes her dentures out and places them on her nightstand and I decide I never want her to leave. She runs her tongue over her gums then slumps. When I walk by to use the bathroom, she tells me I have nice legs and a pretty smile. She tells me I sure could be fast if I wanted to. I blush at this, but Mama smiles and says dementia makes people say off things.

Grandma rises between the three of us, a different woman with spirit. I feel the life running in her—it's hot-blooded—and now I smile too, I reach for her hand. I don't want to get our hopes up, so I push the wave inside me down and stuff it in a blue bottle. Mama sighs while she wraps her hair in a silk scarf then puts her oils on, and I clip my retainer in and cut the light. I wish we had the strength to fly.

Uncle Otis comes by the hotel in the morning to see Mama and shoot the shit. He drives trucks for BI-LO and leaves for weeks at a time, so he's come to say goodbye. We meet him outside the hotel and all sit in the rocking chairs, Grandma too. Her neck is limp again and she stares at a fly fidgeting in motor oil. I say I'm going for a walk and sneak behind the dumpster to see if my boyfriend will text me. I shake the phone, willing sweet nothings. I've been burning through my minutes. I only have a few left and the month isn't halfway through.

I worry Cory is talking to Heather when Otis makes a shadow over me. "What you doing back here?" His mouth is a tight line.

I shrug my shoulders and start playing Snake II. I feel that heat in my face again. He clears his throat and I look up. He meets my eyes.

"You didn't see that the other night."

I stare at his shoes and he shifts his weight on his feet. I spit at the ground. He comes toward me, yanks me by my arm. My phone drops.

"You hear me?"

We take Grandma back to Loretta's house later that day and Mama gives Loretta $500 in a money order and an Outback gift card so she can feed Grandma better. Loretta promises to do so and they hug.

We go to say goodbye to Grandma and we kiss her on her head. I squeeze her shoulders and she smiles at us like a baby searching someone's eyes.

When Mama gets back in the car and drives off she starts losing it, screaming, "*Fuck fuck fuck*," and pulling thin pieces of hair from her crown, wiping her eyes. Grandma can't say her name any more and we know what Loretta will use the money on.

Mama screams so hard, blood vessels burst in her eye whites. I float above the car.

She's having one of her breakdowns again. I start picking at the skin on my lips and find a good, dry piece, right in the middle, that will split the center of me. Still no messages from Cory. We soar through the cotton, and I think of wading in it, lying face down in it. Imagining it like cool water. I want every burr to prick my brown ankles. I press my head to the window wishing it would crack. I'm wishing I could fall out the hatch. I'm wishing Grandma could come stay with us in Tennessee. Every time I've asked, nothing changes. *We can always visit, honey.* Daddy always gives the same low no.

Mama isn't ready to go yet, so we take back roads and plan to break up the drive and rest for the night. She calls this a "girls trip." Mama sticks her hand out the window as she drives along the highway. In her mind she's somewhere else.

We stay the night in the middle of nowhere at a bed and breakfast called the Iris House. The floors creak as we walk to the second level and the furniture is coated in dusty lace doilies. Mama takes her "Zen medicine" and falls asleep with all her good clothes on, mouth wide, sprawled over the polyester quilt with little stitched fish. I stare at the ceiling fan, drift in and out of sleep, and wait until midnight to pull my phone out. Under the sheets my bed glows blue, and I'm smelling on one of those French milled soaps again. I stole three from the La Quinta.

My phone dings. There's a bright buzz. My baby Cory sends me a message that makes my heart jump: *U up?*

My face flushes. I feel my underwear pulse tight. I want to look at my body in the mirror, so I walk to the bathroom and hear the whimpering again. I try to open the door but it's locked. Light spreads from the floor.

So, I lay flat and turn my face to the side. I squint one

eye and see Mama sideways on the white tile, makeup running down her pretty face. She cries, curled up with her knees to her chin, her eyes are empty.

And I can't tell what's worse: me seeing her like this or her knowing I'm watching her fault line spread. But I won't leave her. I stay on the floor, pressing my cheek further in. I look through the crack and don't blink. ✽

THE TRUTH ABOUT GATORS

Rabbi Kadens told me not to mix diazepam and red wine. I took my emergency Valium thirty minutes ago and my chest feels like it's dry-drowning. The room is getting hot and my body sways everywhere, spreading. I want attention.

At Rumorz, some random dances with me and a circle forms where white people are trying to prove they have rhythm. I am dancing on the edge of buffoonery in my maternity leggings (not pregnant, just huge) and brass, ethnic, tassel earrings I hope distract from the sliver of jiggling brown fat under my jaw. I need something to steady me when I look up and find him. My gift. Nothing special. I go in the middle of the "dancers," hopping, hoping he's watching me. My friends don't love it when I get like this. Yes, I think, this boy with knocked knees and a bird-beak chin seems available. That's all I want: someone who's available.

During our therapy sessions, Rabbi Kadens tells me I am not available. He says I'm like a root canal. We got to find the rot. We meet three days a week at the Jewish community center where my mandated DBT counseling is on a sliding scale and people ask me if I am lost. But I am not lost. And I can change.

I am on a *journey* ever since I gently stabbed Mr. Jimmy at the barbeque last month. See, his baby toe kept hanging out the front side of his gator sandals, the nail buttery and curved under like an old orange peel. And I sat there staring at him in my misery and remembered all the times he found me after church in the parlor growing up. And the times in the vestibule after service. And I guess the times in the women's bathroom on the third floor, too.

Every Sunday at Brunswick Eternal Harvest Pentecostal went the same. I looked at his feet while he switched over to me and my mother.

"Earlene, don't you look heavenly. So fine."

"Oh, Jimmy," she'd sigh as they hugged in a saintly way, her arms making an A-frame above his bald, dark head, then settling on his shoulders. Her chest always grazed his thin Faded Glory dress shirt, her nipples hard, alert. Then she'd pinch my side and scoot me to him for a hug.

"Come here, baby girl," he'd always say, smelling like Dollar Store Drakkar Noir. And I'd stand there, stiff as a board, my eyes in a soft-raged glare, my body all too familiar with his puncture. Mr. Jimmy always hugged me too long, his mouth smelling like mothballs above me, his crotch resting like a mound of wet cotton balls against the whole of me.

On the day of the cookout, he really irked me. At twenty-three years old, I thought I was grown enough to let it go, it only happened seven times. And besides, my anger with him stunted me from my blessing, but Jimmy still irked me. He was a ghost slip on my body.

He scratched the silver naps at the back of his head with his pointer fingernail, and I watched his skin fall like ash on his shoulders. We had gone all out: New York Strips we got two for one at the Food Lion. Jimmy said he'd fix 'em right for us. When I first saw the dandruff flakes, I was sure he'd wash his hands, sure he'd scrape the gunk out somehow. The white, cottage cheese–looking shit sat thick on the underside of his long, rounded nail.

But he didn't scrape. He didn't dust his hands off on his pants. He reached over the grill with his bare hands and flipped the meat, then he licked his lips at me.

So, I lost it. Clawed an ice pick from an Igloo cooler and made a few indentions on him. I don't remember much else after. But now I see Rabbi Kadens.

"The health department is two doors down," a woman tells me at the community center one door over from the synagogue. I stare at her and the edges of her lace front wig, and I wonder if she buys her hair from the Asian store on Magnolia, like me.

"I'm here for therapy."

I need her to know I am responsible, as this was my only sensible option. I keep myself accountable. Either twelve sessions or the hospital. She blinks twice. I ask if she knows where Rabbi Kadens' office is. I ask the white way, changing my voice to upper-middle-class, NPR-style vocal fry: brighter As, shorter vowels, tightness on the Ts. I try to show I am in college and can count. She gives a no-teeth smile and points behind her. I smile with all my teeth and gums—*see I have them all*—and walk quickly. I worry I smell like cocoa butter.

In today's session, I am learning about my attachment style. Last week, Rabbi Kadens told me my disorganized style makes me act in an anxious, compulsive manner. In response, I made the mistake of telling Rabbi Kadens my dad moonlighted as a public access televangelist before he died. Now he lays on the God stuff pretty thick. All his breakthrough analogies are from the Book of Samuel.

"See Nicki, I've been thinking, and I *think* I've got you pegged." He rests his fingers on his lips, sits back and crosses his leg.

"You're like King David, you know about him? Remember him and Bathsheba?"

I stare.

"You have delayed reactions *then* you melt!" Rabbi Kadens laughs at this. "I've got a David in my office! Help me! Ahh!"

He guffaws and reaches out to grab my hand, but settles on my bare thigh. I laugh back, my hand flopping on top of his like a dead bass. Our eyes meet until I check the clock; we have twenty minutes left. There's a cold sub sandwich on his desk. The deli meat sweats and I smell the mayonnaise turn. My stomach growls while he does his little wrap-up routine, checks in with me, and checks to see how my anxiety is going.

"And remember the Valium can be habit-forming. Half a pill, if ever. And never with alcohol. Only ever in emergencies. Only if you really need to leave the present moment."

His voice trails while I check the dirt under my nails. Back at my apartment, the chicken salad I left out earlier is probably starting to turn, too. It's summer and by now, the gnats are laying eggs in the neck of the Barefoot wine bottle I left uncorked on the balcony. When I get home, I think, I'll swallow it anyway. Big gulps. And then I think of the rabbi's hand on me, dry and heavy and confident, not basement-damp like I hoped it would be. I think of his feet, too, if I can imagine them correctly. I've never seen them bare; maybe I'd suck the toes. Then I start to wonder if Jewish men wear gators. I wonder if Rabbi Kadens' baby toenail curls under, too.

Club Rumorz smells like baby powder and my inner thighs. Under the lights, his wide smile tells me he's what I need. I feel an innocence radiating, like he cares about doing right by people. This makes me aggressive. I look at him with his spacey, dopey glare while he tells me he goes to school in Vermont. He moves his hands up my stomach, feeling my tits. I worry he feels sweat through my girdle and from his body odor, I can smell that he does, in fact, go to school in Vermont. He dances behind me in his white socks. I don't think he's partial to show-ers, and I can't tell what I want to do with him. This inch of attention consumes me.

He is lanky—every part of his body extends beyond normal. His neck is dignified, stretching tall with an Adam's apple that juts out like half a Cutie tangerine. It's smooth like the porcelain in my bathtub. His jeans have a snag in the crotch that opens to a tiny hole where I see the plaid of his underwear and when the lighting's right, a lump of hairless testicle. It catches my eye, shining like a fishing lure. The more I tell myself not to look, the more I fucking do.

He is eager and offbeat, which sends me spiraling in poetics. I think he feels limited in his own body. He moves in a clumsy grace with eel-like arms, smiling down at me in full, pierced with dimples. He can't dance. And you fuck how you dance. I'm enamored. Pieces of oiled hair flop into his doe eyes. It smells like month-old bed sheets. I want to place my nose in his crown, in a pool of sebum, and inhale it, deeply. I want to rub a portion right into my crow's feet. I want to move a strand back for him, placing it behind his cowish, baby-boy ears.

Purple lights shine around him as we dance and dance and dance, making him look a frumpy kind of holy. He is tall—taller than six feet, at best guess. He wears high waters—tube socks compensate for exposed, bare ankles.

"What's your name?" I ask, beaming.

"Huh?"

"What's YOUR name?"

"You've got a great ass!"

He spins me around, spanks me a little.

I gulp down more of my Shiraz and feel that buzzed heat wave making me wanna tell my truth! Rabbi Kadens says I should do that more. My poise cracks when I put my arms around him. I don't mean to, but I pull on his neck too long. His eyes are moony with cringe. I spill wine down his back. Whitney Houston comes on, and I try to lock eyes to share a moment. I offer him some of my drink but he doesn't take it—he says he doesn't want to take my wine from me. I gawk at him for this, mouth open, like the gesture feels beyond gracious, and he picks at his thumbs and looks away from me. He's nervous.

I want him to be nervous. Really, I'm making him uncomfortable. He starts to soak with sweat: a glisten that makes his body gloss under the LEDs. But now the sweat takes on a drenching effect, pouring through his hair and down his neck, making him look like a newborn calf. A couple drops splash on my face when he lifts his arms and screams, "WOOH I love this song!"

I try to lick them off of him when he pulls his head back from me and says he needs some water. I watch his shoulders square as he goes to the bar. In my mind, he's pulling me into the bathroom, ripping my control-top leggings down, licking at the pink of me. But he's not looking at me. He won't look at me. And now he's dancing with some other girl with a belly button ring, golden retriever lowlights, a flat stomach. I lose sight of him altogether. They turn the black lights on and everybody glows. I keep searching for him, trying to smell him in the air.

I'm pacing the floor when J pulls me aside and tells me it's time to go cause, apparently, I'm clowning myself. I tell her she's clowning because I forgot I even came here with friends.

"Nicki, girl, this doesn't look good on you," she says, as she pulls me back by the waist. I roll my neck at her with my arms crossed and slur to her something about how Mr. Jimmy didn't expect me to cut his Black, dusty ass.

"Who's Jimmy?" She wipes runny lipstick off my chin.

She goads me, lets me know I'm embarrassing myself. I'm too deflated to protest so I let her pull me back through the crowd. But I keep looking for my one good thing.

When I finally find him I wave from across the room. He looks through me, but I tell myself he couldn't handle the passion. 'Cause we had a cosmic connection. Star crossed. We had a cosmic connection. I'm sure of it. The floor feels like water as J starts to pull me toward the exit.

In the Uber, I pick my skin around my thumbs and suck out the little pools as I let the coastal Georgia wind whip my face. I look out the window searching for a glimmer, only to be let down by a flat night. It's cloudy; no full moon, no one thousand glittering stars, just a wet rush on my face, too dark to see.

I look off toward the port and wave to the shipping boats, pointing to each of them as if I know them by name. I make sure they feel seen and heard. I tell myself I'm a good person. My eyes water from the wind and my kohl liner gives me coon circles. I wipe off the black smut and suck it off my fingers.

I don't wanna feel so down anymore, so I beg the driver for a hit off her cotton candy vape and imagine my lungs combusting above me. It tastes how Mr. Jimmy smells. I feel his fingernails. I feel his hands around my throat. I feel his palm pushing my head down. I see myself on my knees. I was so little then.

I start laughing. I yank my head around and tell a BIG story about the random to my friends in the back seat, fishing for some approval. "And then he went down on me in the bathroom!" They laugh with ("at," I hear the rabbi say) me, egging me on, and I feel better. J pats my shoulder.

The Eagles play on 91.9, "The Soft Rock Choice of Chatham County," and I think of the sandwich on Rabbi

Kadens' desk. It's probably still sitting there. I get to ripping through my pockets for his number, pulling the white, inside parts all the way out. I'm swooning, floating on stale hope, thinking I really met somebody, even though I know.

Mr. Jimmy will still be at the service on Sunday. Most of the men I know wear gators, and I'm a wishing fool: I'll never see my random again.

But I try. I stick my head back out the window and send him a message, I reach through the void. And I think he got it, 'cause I closed my eyes when I wished. ✳

HUNGRY

To stay out of the pantry on a Friday night, I went downstairs to smoke out of the big corner window. It was the last week of May, the last week of my miserable eighth grade year, and come fall, I'd be in high school. Daddy was still in the hospital recovering from surgery and would be released in a week or so—a few days before my graduation. I was fiddling for my cigarettes, about to reach the bottom step, when I heard panting like dogs in heat. Ms. Glenda straddled both sides of my Mother's hips, her hair was wet with sweat. My mother was crying. Ms. Glenda cupped her hand under my mother's chin and kissed her eyes. I turned around and snuck back upstairs while one of them moaned like she wasn't hiding in our basement. Daddy didn't need any more shock. I sucked my stomach in then pushed it all down deep.

"Bad blood," as Aunt Esther called it, ran on both sides of our family. It crept up on Daddy last year, and despite the warnings, all it took was a pin-prick wound for him to come undone. In March, he developed gout, then in April nerve damage—neuropathy—in that same foot; it started to tingle and then he lost most of the feeling altogether. Then in early May the back of his heel got cut, nothing more than a scrape. He didn't feel it, and soon after it got infected and turned into an open sore that turned gangrene, which traveled up the appendage, which led to his foot getting cut off at the ankle.

This all led to me going to my first meeting before eighth grade even let out for summer. As soon as I saw Daddy come into our house with bandages where his foot used to be, I knew someone had to change.

Aunt Esther wanted me to keep my vitality early in life. "You're too young for all this weight. I know we run big, but you have to get slim," she told me a million times. She prodded me to the meetings for months. I hadn't wanted to go. I couldn't imagine going to another place where people judged my body. But I'd finally caved. I thought of Aunt Esther as more of a mother than my own. She looked more like me and Daddy anyway.

I looked out the window while Aunt Esther listened to Destiny's Child on low. We drove twenty minutes down a country road to Second United Methodist, a cold, castle-type church with white Jesus in stained glass. Aunt Esther tapped her thumbs on the steering wheel and cleaned some waffle from in between her teeth. She took me to breakfast at Denny's earlier in the morning for one last hoorah. We wore matching airbrush T-shirts from our spring break trip to Ruby Falls. I felt excited about the new me; I imagined the fat melting off my waist like butter.

"Are you nervous?" Aunt Esther asked in the car. Her stomach bubbled around the seatbelt.

"No, not really."

"It's okay if you are. This is a safe space. No one will judge you." She looked over at me and patted my shoulder. I didn't believe her but it felt good to be in her car, just us, moving away from home.

"Eh, I feel fine." I looked out the window and saw a picket sign: WEIGHT WATCHERS SLIM DOWN! TURN HERE.

"Well, here we go. If at any time you feel uncomfortable, let me know. Squeeze my hand three times, and we'll leave. You hear me?"

I nodded and slowly made my way out the door and into the basement's rec room.

I knew I had to get smaller for two reasons.

The first reason: For him. Last summer the doctor gave him the diagnosis. They'd been warning him about it for years. His daddy had it, his daddy's daddy had had it, and so on. The doctor told our family Daddy would have to change his lifestyle tremendously or things could turn quick: lost eyesight, kidney problems, cirrhosis, lost limbs, heart attack, even stroke. As the doctor drilled him, I looked over at my father and saw strong parts of me reflected back: his smooth pecan face, long legs, broad shoulders, and dark eyelashes. I looked back at my mother: so fit, her eyes severe, disappointed. I wondered what would become of us.

When Mom brought Daddy home from his surgery, he tried to have some humor about it. He made jokes about himself having been All-American, a Wharton bigwig, the strongest star length softball coach, and whatnot. "Now look at me," he said.

Neighbors visited and brought us food after the procedure. They made low-carb stews and veggie stir-fries. Glenda came over too and offered to be helpful: "Just tell me what to do, whatever you need." She brought a sugar-free angel food cake, hugged all of us with a bony warmth, and wiped down our counters. She said she would be there as much as she could to help out. She and my mother barely made eye contact, and I wondered if I really saw what I remembered.

The second reason: I had something to prove. My mother eternally harped on me about my weight, nagging me, squishing my sides, only letting me have my sweets on special occasions. Her body weighed her down so she couldn't imagine mine as anything other than a burden. I'd never seen her face bare. She touched up her makeup before going to bed and believed in preventative Juvederm at the ripe age of thirty-five. Any time I whined about feeling insecure, she put a hand to my face and scoffed, "You think you have it bad, you just don't know." As a child, on Saturdays, her mother woke her and her sisters up and brought them to the laundry room in their white sleep slips. She placed them on top of their yellow top load Maytag, then started an empty wash cycle. As the machine moved, she circled where they jiggled—"improvement areas," she called them.

Mom had been hospitalized twice for anorexia in high school. Ran so long and so hard she'd permanently lost the cartilage in her knees—at forty she had already had the left one replaced. Outside of her food issues, she felt effervescent—smart, funny, larger than life—but between the two of us, because I wasn't the size she needed me to be, she felt bitter, mean about food, and mad about me. "Ten more pounds and she'll roll," I heard her say to her sister on the phone. She'd even taped WordArt reminders on my bathroom mirror and above the left door handle on the fridge: "NOTHING TASTES AS GOOD AS THIN FEELS."

And she wasn't the only one. It seemed like everybody had something to say about my big bones: my teachers, my friends' mothers, the mailman. Earlier this year, at Katie Castellano's sleepover, after we played light as a feather, stiff as a board, we played a new game called "guess how much," where each of the girls got on the scale in Katie's mother's bathroom while the others wrote on slips of paper how much they thought the girl on the scale weighed. We folded the slips of paper and placed them in a fishbowl, then watched with wide eyes while she stepped on and the numbers calibrated. Even the girl getting weighed herself would step on the scale backward, and someone would hold the fishbowl out to her and she would drop her guess in the bowl, too. After we saw the number, Katie would scoop out the guesses and stand in front of us and read us our weight. Whoever guessed closest won. Of course, the real winner weighed the least. My self-estimate? Fifteen pounds too generous, and I lost the game by about forty pounds. I stood there with them watching me in silence, mortified.

Walking into the meeting, I barely noticed anyone around me. Instead, my whole body focused on shrinking.

"ARE YOU HUNGRY FOR LIFE?" Neon-pink, Comic Sans flyers interrogated me across the walls.

Aunt Esther walked me to the check-in counter to get measured, and I tucked in line behind her.

The acrylics on the check-in lady's hand were perfect, so pink. The French tips were sharply squared and bright, bleach-white. The gloss on them looked wealthy. The way they sat on her hands looked so familiar, and I realized they were the same ones I saw running down my mother's brown back in the basement.

"Welcome to the first day of your new life!" Glenda said to me and Aunt Esther while shaking our hands. I felt clammy against her lotioned palm.

Hospitality reeked out of Glenda, those bright teeth stark against her shiny skin. Tide detergent wafted off her body and into my face while I looked at her, my eyes narrow with knowing, and she glanced back at me, just a nobody. Ms. Glenda signed me in and made me a name tag, then gave me my introductory packet.

WELCOME TO THE NEW YOU! it said on the glossy outside, with a photo of a slim Asian woman smiling while eating a forkful of salad. I opened it and filled out the questionnaire.

> On a scale of 1 to 10, how much does food control your life? 10
> On a scale of 1 to 10, how motivated do you feel to exercise? 3
> On a scale of 1 to 10, how would you rate your self-esteem, right now? 2
> On a scale of 1 to 10, how attached do you feel to sugar? 10
> One a scale of 1 to 10, how much are you ready to change (p.s. The only acceptable answer is 10!)? 10

After I filled it out, Ms. Glenda took my pamphlet and told me when it was my turn to step on the scale.

"What about my clothes?"

I wondered if anything I was wearing had been in the pile on the laundry room floor that night.

"Yes, ma'am! You're a smart one. We take off four pounds in place of being fully clothed. That's the one great thing about these meetings—you can always count on losing four pounds!" She winked and gestured for me to step on. Her smell slapped me in the face again.

I looked down expecting to see a number, but the screen was taped over with pink construction paper that read YOU ARE BEAUTIFUL! with heart stickers plastered around. Ms. Glenda looked at my weight on the computer screen and tapped it with her shiny index nail. She bit her lip a little, then smiled, scribbled some numbers in my pamphlet, and ushered me into the big meeting room with a skylight the size of heaven.

Aunt Esther and I sat together in the third row from the back after we grabbed our refreshments. There were maybe twenty other women, mostly Aunt Esther's age. A few pudgy twentysomethings lurked in the back rows. I kept wondering if I was crazy; if I was sure I saw Ms. Glenda a few nights before, in between my mother's legs. I went to get something to drink.

I saw lemonade. The meeting was off to a great start. It was Crystal Light, raspberry flavored, and Ms. Glenda and the other leaders cut up individual Atkins bars into mini baking cups: the option of "mocha mint" or "peanut butter chocolate chip" for us all to choose.

The meeting started with the Slideshow of Success. Ms. Glenda came up to the front, but this time she was what my father would call "deadly serious." With the clicker in her hand, she turned the projector on, and it opened to a photo of her pushing 300 pounds. Then she pressed the clicker and showed another one of her after she lost 150 of them. She preached to us about the importance of self-responsibility.

"It's all about willpower."

"Only YOU can make the change."

The room erupted in clapping for Ms. Glenda while she mouthed, "Thank you, thank you," over and over again, with her hand on her chest. From my seat I counted four of her ribs. All of us newbies were hooked, as she talked about how Weight Watchers gave her ownership over all the areas of her life she couldn't control; it gave her a sense of strength. I was burning in my seat, ready for my miracle.

After the presentation, there was a part of the meeting where anyone could walk up to the microphone in the middle of the room and testify about their program successes. One woman, Daisy, stood up and said she lost her first five pounds. She lifted her shirt and tugged at the waistband of her khakis to show us the slack. Everyone gasped, which made her smile and caused her to lean into the mic closer.

"How were you able to do it, girl?" Aunt Esther asked from the audience. I hated how friendly she could be.

"Sticking to my low-point foods, and substituting sugar-free everything! It's all about low carb for me!"

Ms. Glenda came up beside her and congratulated Daisy by rubbing her shoulders and whispering in her ear. Daisy beamed.

I took mental notes on everything I learned that day: drinking hot water could make you feel fuller longer; Parkay Butter Spray was program friendly; sugar-free Jello with unsweetened whipped cream could fill the fructose hole; and, perhaps most important, being fat was the worst thing any woman could ever be.

At my graduation ceremony, Mom and Daddy and Aunt Esther sat close to the stage and waved to me when it was my turn to walk across. Mom was there taking pictures of me, the flash bright from the wind-up camera she bought just an hour before at the corner store. Daddy sat in his chair and clapped for me the loudest, wearing a bow tie the same shade of purple as my middle school. I felt embarrassed in my women's size-eight dress. All my friends were still in pre-teen sizes. I already wore a B-cup bra.

Daddy had been ordered by the doctor to stay in his wheelchair, and me and Mom tried a million different ways to hide his loss. We couldn't afford any type of decent prosthetic in our wildest dreams, so we did the next best thing and got crafty. We tried filling his slacks with tufts of stuffing and attached his dress shoe at the bottom, but it wouldn't hold. Eventually, we made the painful decision to cut his pant leg and bind it right below where the ankle would have been, securing it with a black rubber band.

As I walked across, he smiled from ear to ear, but when I looked over at him again his face had dropped, his shoulders were drooped, and he was wiping tears away. I couldn't tell if they were the kind that came from great pride or unbearable grief.

When summer break finally started, Aunt Esther and I went to Weight Watchers every week. I had a goal to lose thirty-five pounds before high school that fall, and she dreamt of losing fifteen. I begged Mom to help me buy better foods and fill the fridge with them, which pleased her. I ate steamed broccoli and cod with lemon pepper, stopped having added sugar, and only drank water if I couldn't get a diet soda.

The weight fell off pretty quickly. Daddy got worse.

With his illness rocketing since the amputation, they placed him on injectable insulin. The vials sat in the fridge next to my Gatorade Zero, and every morning, I watched him drink his coffee, then pinch a fold on the side of his stomach while he jabbed the clear liquid into himself.

Daddy's days seemed perpetually dreary. He became obsessed with the statistics against him. Wheeling around the kitchen, he would say them out loud over and over again: *Black men have a 50 percent chance in developing diabetes over any other group of people. People with diabetes are two times more likely to get depression. People who get an amputation from a diabetes complication have a 75 percent rate of losing another body part.*

He couldn't shake it. He and my mother would fight about it. She called him pessimistic. He said he was accepting of the inevitable.

I didn't understand how it changed so quickly, how he could have let himself get this bad. It started last year, when he got laid off from his C-suite job. He came home different. Before this he seemed perfect; my safe, reliable, Disney movie father. A good dad, he ran two miles a day, wore the same dry-cleaned clothes, told dumb jokes, took the cars to get the oil changed. We would take walks sometimes in the evenings, get ice cream, and watch Turner Classic Movies. But one day he gave up. And no matter how much I asked about what happened, no one would tell me why.

After he got the diagnosis last summer, Daddy and Mom started sleeping in separate rooms. Mom started slamming doors. And he started staying at home more. He quit asking if I wanted to run to the store with him and stopped prodding at me to get off the computer. He came home late, and drank Black and Tans on the couch. Some days, I'd tried to get him to go with me down by the dock and watch the water to cheer him up, but all he wanted was his time. He got so thirsty all of a sudden and went through pints of iced tea, complained of exhaustion, and kept rushing to the restroom.

Daddy became erratic. His moods made him throw his pill bottles against the wall in the kitchen, weep uncontrollably, or become withdrawn. Most days he would sit on the couch with his crutches laid to the side and watch Lifetime movies with a flat look in his eye.

Ms. Glenda was winning. Ms. Glenda was ruining my family. Ms. Glenda from down the street, married with two kids, was lying to my father's face. Ms. Glenda, head of the cross-country team parent association with Revlon blonde hair, was sleeping with my mother and didn't feel bad about it.

I dragged myself across the world that summer. I was too young for a gym membership, so I started walking everywhere. At Weight Watchers, Ms. Glenda mentioned getting a pedometer and walking 10,000 steps a day, so I upped mine to 19,000. I walked laps in the back-yard with my Discman and sports bra. Back and forth, I turned golden in the summer sun. I watched myself in the reflection off our sliding glass door and hoped I could whittle away.

I made a friend in the meetings, Rachel Goldstein, who was a rising sophomore and lived in Sequoia Hills. She had lost forty-seven pounds the summer before. Every morning, she started coming over and pacing with me, both of us wearing matching Puma sweatbands while we talked about periods and third base and how to check our BMIs. She also taught me about sugar-free gum and how to vomit with the back of a toothbrush. Under the dogwood trees, while we sweated, she told me stories about her new twenty-three-year-old boyfriend, Johnny, and the vibrator he bought her from Spencer's.

While we paced and paced, Daddy wasted. Despite his reluctance, me and Mom lugged him to the doctor as often as we could, and we learned the new medication had a potential side effect of major depressive disorder.

Most evenings he sat around, dumbstruck, in an SWV T-shirt he wore for a few days straight, collar stretched out. Mom was nowhere to be found in the evenings, running her endless list of errands. She was nicer to me, would see me around, put her hands on my waist, squeezing, and say, "Finally, there's my pretty girl," in passing as we went our separate ways. I lost track of the days altogether.

I slept over at Rachel's house as much as possible. I was sick of seeing my dad so pitiful, and I was obsessed with disappearing. Her house was exactly three miles away, so I walked to it as much as I could. It was nice to have a best friend. Rachel's parents divorced a few years earlier, so just her father and she lived there. Mr. Goldstein worked bi-coastally for a Fortune 500 consulting firm, which left Rachel mostly alone, save for her 7,000-square-foot home and her nanny Delores, who drank Rolling Rock beers and watched *Days of Our Lives* while she rested her eyes.

Before Aunt Esther picked us up for the meetings, Rachel and I went to her bathroom and made ourselves throw up anything in our stomachs. After, we took a tape measure to our waists. Hers stayed at nineteen inches, mine not budging at twenty-one. On bad days she'd hold my hand or put an arm around me. "We'll do better tomorrow." My throat burned with bile like I'd swallowed the sun.

On good days, while Aunt Esther blew on the horn, we would look at ourselves in the mirror and sling our arms around each other, taking turns, standing hip bone to hip bone, calling one another "simply divine."

Mom and Aunt Esther started talking a lot in other rooms when I was home. They would whisper so quietly, making hushed noises in the guest room, then come out, wiping their eyes quickly.

Other than doctor appointments, Dad hadn't left the house in seven weeks.

My breath smelled perpetually sour, and I wore heavy black clothes all day in the sun to make me sweat as much as possible. One day when I walked over to Rachel's estate, Delores opened the door and wouldn't pull it past the chain lock. "Rachel's not having company right now. She's out of town." She glared at me. I asked when she would get back, and Delores told me not for a long while. It turned out Rachel's dad was more in tune than we expected, and she had been filling him in on our concerning behavior. Delores handed me a glossy brochure for the Young Roses Treatment Facility for Anorexia Nervosa and Bulimia, told me to please take care of myself, then shut the door. They had sent Rachel away to the West Coast campus in Malibu. I stood there for a while and stared at placid pictures of a rocky beach and the big, blue Pacific.

That night, Mr. Goldstein called our landline and said Rachel wouldn't be talking to me for a while. He asked me to put one of my parents on the phone, but I told him my parents were never home.

School started soon, and I beat my goal: I lost around forty pounds from May to September and mastered any type of pangs with my mints and cigarettes on the hour.

Fluid ballooned around Daddy's ankle and his wrists. I could hear him breathing or trying to breathe, his mouth wide and gasping as he complained all day of his tongue feeling like chalk. He wouldn't even move from the couch, sometimes for almost two days. When I would ask him, "Daddy, don't you need to use the restroom?" he would chuckle and say, "Actually, dear, I don't. Even if I wanted to piss, nothing would come out."

The last time we ate dinner as a family, Mom and Daddy asked me if I was happy about going to high school with my new buddy soon. I shrugged.

He quit eating. I cried myself to sleep.

Aunt Esther was the one to finally tell me it was kidney failure. She was taking me to my final Weight Watchers meeting of the summer, a week before school started, and I was smacking sugar-free Dentyne Ice, imagining it as a whole cheese pizza. When Aunt Esther missed the turn to the Methodist church, I figured she wasn't paying attention. She kept driving up the parkway. I figured we were going someplace else. We pulled over at a stop to watch the mountains, and we got out and sat on a bench, the same one we would come to from time to time when I was a child.

"Now dear, I need to tell you something," she said.

"Okay."

"Your father, he isn't doing too well."

"Mhmm."

"Okay. So, listen good and hard to me. He is in acute kidney failure and only has a few months left to live, if he can't get a transplant."

"Mhmm." I reached for my pedometer. Only 9,000 steps so far, *shit*. It should have been around 15k. I'd been up since five that morning running the numbers: pacing, doing crunches, hopping on and off and on and off the scale.

"The transplant list has so many people on it, it is not likely that he will get one in time. Do you understand what I'm saying to you?"

My ears started to ring, and I felt full from my chest to my toes. I shoved four pieces of gum in the back of my mouth, and a piece of foil caught in between the pieces.

"I'm so sorry, sweetie. We didn't know how to tell you. I wish I would have told you sooner, but your mom and I were in total shock."

A few days later, I went to drop a postcard off for Rachel at the mailbox, and I was trying to enjoy the breeze in my hair, trying to think of him with me. Daddy liked summer. He used to take me for sunset walks in the summer.

When I got back in the house, I thought Daddy was just asleep, so I didn't bother him. I walked over to him and pulled the blanket up to his shoulders and cut the TV off. He looked okay, peaceful really, and I felt punched in the gut when I looked at him lying there on our old leather sectional. I thought of our summers on the Outer Banks, looking for creatures in the low tide at night, buckets in our hands and stars above us. How could this be the same man who held me above the waves until I loved the water as much as he did? I thought about calling out my mother's name to see if she was around. I checked the fridge to test myself and saw a note she left. OUT WITH GIRLFRIENDS FOR DINNER. TXT IF YOU NEED ME!

I needed to make sure that Daddy took his meds, so I went to wake him up and that's when I realized how hard it was for him to breathe. He wheezed like a fish, his lips turned blue.

I was the only one who rode with him in the ambulance.

Aunt Esther made it there right as they put the intubation tubes in. They were able to get him stable, but soon after they placed him in a coma so his body could regulate. For a man who seemed unbreakable, he looked impossibly weak as he lay hooked up to machines that breathed for him. The doctor said he might be able to improve temporarily, but not for long. With his need for the transplant and this damage to his immune system, our days together were numbered. I kept waiting for Daddy to open his eyes.

Everything was about willpower. My wants were just an illusion to be managed.

Any cravings signaled a deeper need.

When I wanted sugar, I really needed fruit.

When I was craving salt, I really just felt thirsty.

The trick was to master my desire, that's what I learned in the meetings. I needed to trick my mind. You gotta know when you're really hungry and when you just think you are.

It was nearly an hour after we arrived when Ms. Glenda and my mother showed up to the hospital. My eyes burned out of my skull in rage. Mom was beside herself, demanding to know the details, fat tears down her face: Where was he when I found him? Did he take his insulin? Did I check on him? *Selfish*, she called me. She acted a fool in the hospital room, sobbing, then yelling, then sobbing again, while my father laid stiff on those starchy hospital sheets.

Ms. Glenda came over to my mother and held her tenderly, leaned her whole body against her and whispered something in my mother's ear. She held onto the back of her neck, and moved the hair out of her face.

"You've gotta be fucking kidding me," Aunt Esther sighed, standing. She paced the room.

But my mother didn't even look at her, and kept holding on to Ms. Glenda for support. Ms. Glenda heard it, though.

"Esther, I can't imagine what you're going through. I promise I'm here." She looked over at him with puppy eyes.

My aunt started saying something about her nerve, but a nurse walked in and she stopped.

I walked over to Daddy and tried to feel the warmth in his hands. I squeezed three times, hoping he'd squeeze back and let me know this was one of his jokes, that he was ready to go home. My mother continued to wail into Ms. Glenda's arms, and I kept squeezing, trying to move the life back into him.

The nurse checked his oxygen line. She looked at us. I froze like I was running in quicksand. She checked his pulse, and made some notes, then left without saying anything. The doctor came in and said he had to share some news.

Aunt Ester pulled me away.

"We should get some fresh air, baby," she cooed. "That sounds nice, right? Come on with me, let's take a break."

I checked my pedometer: only 11,000. I needed to take a few more. Together, we walked out past my mother and Ms. Glenda, down the stairs, out the exit doors and into the dark night.

I kept thinking about what Glenda taught us in that first seminar (was that really a few months ago?): how to keep it off, the BIG secret. Aunt Ester had tried that day to grab my hand in the pew, but I'd moved it away from her while I zeroed in and held my breath. Glenda kept telling us it was all in the mind.

Nothing tastes as good as thin feels.

Did Glenda tell this to my mother? Or did my mother tell it to her?

You must change. You can disappear.

You have to find the will to fill the void, then make it so. ✳

SKIN HUNGER

While baby fever spread among our small group, I knew I'd never have one with my husband John.

"Mary-Martha's having a girl," he told me. Mary-Martha was married to John's best friend, Waylon, a tax lawyer. Lately, she'd been keeping her ring hand on her stomach a lot, especially in conversation with unmarried women. She was having the nursery done in West Elm. Shelbey, the Waldorf school teacher, was expecting as well, just a month behind Mary-Martha. She married Tommy, who just finished his optometry residence. Naomi couldn't get pregnant. She and her husband, Devin, weren't talking much because of it. Devin resented her barren womb and was in therapy with our minister's brother to figure out how to let that go.

All women hosted rotating bi-weekly wine nights, and I tried to fit in with them as best as I could.

Our small group, the Young Adults Study Group of Christ the Savior Presbyterian, signaled pseudo-prestige in the Knoxville community. As well connected as any country club, all of the other couples were white and ranged from upper-middle-class to wealthy, with the husbands graduating with degrees in supply chain management and eventually taking post-graduation jobs with Deloitte or Volkswagen. Having children—preferably many—was another way to be part of the club.

The group we were with wasn't very religious, but it had a purpose. We gathered with the intent to talk about community, friendship, marriage, and spiritual disciplines. We got *almost* wasted a few times a week and talked about the weather.

Most visits revolved around the home and things within the home: the couches, flooring, and general cleanliness. The nonstop rearranging and redecorating could make a woman feel like she could not keep up. Last week we all went to Alice and Michael's. Her husband and she had been trying for three years and no sign of luck. What felt like failure fueled her digs. With a simple glance, she could make a person reconsider their entire sense of self-esteem. At our house, she stared at the baseboards I never cleaned and talked about the new "pure mama" non-toxic cleaning supplies she'd been making with thieves oil and white vinegar.

Alice had laser precision and incredible influence. If she made an aside about someone's hair color growing out, that young woman would—the next day—frantically get a touch up, only for Alice to comment on how the colorist always gets it almost right.

I felt like I could never get it right with them, or me and him.

As an engineer, John thought the problem of my infertility was all-around planning. He started tracking my cycle on his phone and asked me to check my cervical fluid in the morning. Every failed pregnancy test created a minefield for days after. John would be cold, dismissive, keeping to himself until I was ovulating, then he was curled at my back, ready to give it another go. I felt like a breeding cow, not a wife.

I wasn't getting pregnant because I was still on birth control. I was planning to tell him but just hadn't found the right time.

In a couple weeks, my big sister, Vanessa, was having a retirement party from the post office, and I needed a place to stay. I was an accident, a late in life "surprise," putting her and I seventeen years apart. My sister moved to Monteagle when I was ten to take a job in a one-room post office. She'd made it clear early in life: She did what she wanted when she wanted. At twenty-one, she started a high-yield savings account, in part, to save enough to afford getting her tubes tied. When she did, my parents were devastated—no grandchild from their firstborn—but guilt didn't work on Vanessa. She came first in her life.

"Y'all need the quaint life," she'd tell us at Christmas when our family complained about how busy we all were. I was excited for a chance to go plan a party for her, to be with people from home. I lay with John in our bed and searched for hotels. We agreed I could go off the grid this trip and unwind—no cell phone, no group chat, just me.

"I want you to take this time and really think about us. Think about how full our lives will be with this baby. Pray on this," he said.

"Okay honey, absolutely."

"'Cause I read stress has a lot to do with fertility issues."

"So do demanding husbands." I smiled and patted him on the thigh.

"You're always joking about this, but it's serious to me. I've wanted our baby for a while now and it's not happening, and I'm not sure why."

"Any other orders, sir?" I saluted him. He rubbed my back.

I planned to book a rental within a fifteen-minute drive to my sisters. John reminded me I must think of our whole future family with the cost. Even a couple hundred dollars could be used efficiently or frivolously. The cost of my stay could become a nicer baby crib or money we could use for diapers.

Money was not an issue, and it never had been. We both earned good salaries. He still pulled from a trust fund. But I agreed and said of course, of course. John was an old-money boy, but in recent years he had taken to frugality. We now were a one-car couple; we stopped eating out unless it was with friends, and he had alerts set up to go to his phone anytime I used my debit card. Every extra cent would go toward our future family.

I met John through his sister, Allie, my OneLife leader from high school.

My family and I were new members at Christ the Savior, looking for a different congregation. My mom and dad left our old church when I was sixteen because they needed a church with "more community focus," which was code for higher social capital. They pushed me to get involved in the youth group. I'd been feeling sadder and sadder and could only explain it to them by saying it felt like I was floating—like I rose above my life and was observing instead of participating in it. My parents wanted me to feel connected again to my faith before I left for Vanderbilt. I just wanted to feel something.

After I'd finally come to Christ, after the Baptism and after Allie said, "I knew I'd get you eventually," she invited me to her parents' thirty-fifth wedding anniversary, and that was where I first met John. We barely spoke. When his mother asked me to throw away her dinner plate for her, Allie cleared her throat and said, "Mom, this is Shauna, my *friend*." My future mother in law smiled without apologizing and told me how much she liked my hair. I'd recently gotten a Keratin treatment, and it was slicked straight to my head. "I like this style best on you brown girls. So silky and flowy. Very professional. Looks good with your skin."

The next year, I ran into John at Vandy. We were at the Hill, our local western bar, gross and sticky. His roommate, John David, was known around campus for going up to girls and asking *can I finger you* just to see what happened. From what I'd heard, he had a surprisingly high success rate. He asked me by the Ariat boot DJ booth—said he'd always wanted to see a one like mine— "Is it pink or brown?" He grinned. I threw my drink in his face and hit him in his windpipe. When the bouncer in cowboy boots threw me out, John met me outside. He walked me back to my dorm, kept apologizing, and said his roommate deserved it. I told him about how I'd met his mom already. He laughed. I didn't.

Our current cohort loved being a *group*. They reveled in connection: meetups at breweries, hushed prayers in Panera, bonding at 7 a.m. barre classes. The competition of thinness was the most brutal between the women but the men delighted in their own disordered eating competitions with intermittent fasting and no-carb weeks. We kept up, for the most part, settling comfortably in second or third place. John would be taking over his father's consulting business in about a year after he retired. I was up for a promotion at the office, training for a 10k and debating on curtain or straight bangs. But the one thing we didn't have was a baby.

John was so ready. It was all he talked about. It was something that I initially adored about him, his desire for a family. But I was indifferent about having a child. Privately, I leaned more toward not wanting them at all. That conviction deepened with each new baby in the small group. When they got drunk enough, they talked about compromise—how when you find the one, you'll concede on the very thing you were certain you never would. Alice, for instance, never thought she'd have a sofa any color other than white. And she'd been pre-med.

Having the baby felt like a compromise to me. Or, having John's baby. I couldn't stop thinking about who he was, what he thought of me, why he'd married me, and why I married him.

Before we got married, we had a joint bachelor party and everyone went around the table at Regas talking about John and fun memories of him. They kept bringing up something called talent night but John always changed the subject. I ordered him another round of drinks and tried to press harder. "Babe, come on, what's this about?" His face turned beet-bright. Mary-Martha giggled. William, his optometrist friend, started scratching under his arm like a monkey. John wouldn't look me in the eye. One friend pulled out his phone and wagged it in his face, then swatted it away. I snatched his phone out of his hand, turned my back, and zoomed in. It was a picture of a teenage boy in a Michael Jackson "Thriller" costume with minstrel makeup. Under his jerry curl wig, his lips were outlined in peach, and his face was as dark as coffee grinds. I looked up, and John buried his head in his hands.

William rubbed my shoulders. "We always knew you went that way! It came too natural to ya. You got a pretty one, boy," he said. They hollered again.

John looked at me, and I looked down at the phone again. The photo was taken from their yearbook. Under the photo were the words *John Thompson Grade 12 Running Back*. John's smile was ear to ear. The belt on his costume was a red, white, and blue bedazzled Stars and Bars flag.

I should have known better. I think I did. When we first started dating, John mentioned to me a lot that while I was Black, I wasn't *Black* Black.

That night, we walked back to the car in silence, drove home in silence, and laid in the bed in silence. I rolled over on my side and shut the lights off and waited. "Please don't take it like that. Don't be that way. I was young and ignorant. I was stupid." He ran his hands across my stomach and kissed my ear. Eventually, I rolled over, and he climbed on top of me.

At a brewery meetup with our friends, I suspected I was missing out on the baby thing. In WASP world, it was the key, and that type of safety would feel good. I clenched my kegel muscles. How many eggs did I even have left? I had no idea what I wanted, but I just wanted something that was mine. I looked at all the couples. They talked; a few played cornhole. To me, everybody had a whole life they were working toward, and I wanted in on my own.

When we were dating and thinking of spending our lives together, I mentioned I might want to have one child in my late thirties. John supported me at the time, but I was soon to be thirty, and I wasn't seeing his vision right. To him, it shifted.

After a round of flip cup, the girls told me how cute I'd look as a mother, how they wondered how curly the baby's hair would look, if she would be caramel like me or pale like her daddy. John put his arm around my shoulders and told them we were trying. They jumped up and down around me.

This was the last month, according to my obstetrician, we would go at it on our own before seeing a fertility specialist. None of them knew I was still on birth control.

My sister knew. I ended up asking her if she knew anyone I could stay with. On the phone, Vanessa paused, confused as to why I wasn't allowed to stay in a hotel. Vanessa's house was tiny, and both of us felt okay with wanting our own space, so she didn't understand what the big deal about getting a hotel room was. After some searching, Vanessa said a co-worker was looking for a house sitter for a few days while she went camping in Oregon.

My sister worked for over twenty years at the Monteagle Post Office and was thrilled to earn a pension that would let her keep her house and snowbird at Rosemary Beach. My trip to see her would be the first time in years I had a moment completely to myself. I'd be there Friday to Friday, the longest time I'd been away from Knoxville and John in six years. The owner said another tenant, a preservationist at Sewanee, rented out the carriage loft next door. The laundry unit was shared and located in the house where I was staying.

"Neil won't bother you! He has a really sweet dog!"

She'd attached his picture in the email for some reason. He looked like John with a beard.

I couldn't make it out of town before Allie came for a visit. We had to do a family dinner night and it fell on small group night, so everyone came to our house. We catered barbecue and had a fire going in the backyard because I told John I couldn't plan my trip and cook. He was embarrassed and insisted we still eat on our nice serv-ingware, not the paper plates that came with the food.

We were all out back, when Allie clinked the side of her White Claw to get our attention. Allie always called me an anomaly and liked to relate to me by sharing her testimony.

"I hadn't even seen a Black person until I went to Jamaica."

I'd heard this one before, a lot: about how until Allie Thompson's sophomore year of college, she'd never said more than a few words in passing to a Black person. During a mission trip to Loving Arms, a Montego Bay orphanage, that changed. She started looking at people differently; considered fate. Her heart stirred when she left the orphanage every day to return to the resort hotel the church put the youth group in.

"It was haunting. I was haunted." Naomi, who was now in her rotation for neonatal care at Ft. Sanders Hospital, gasped. Mary-Martha was already crying, and Allie hadn't even gotten to the juicy parts yet. Shelbey was fanning herself. Alice looked like she was taking notes.

Allie talked often about how *haunted* she was that she couldn't hold them. Haunted as if they were ghosts. The children at Loving Arms experienced "skin hunger," a result of inconsistent touch. Due to overstaffing, lack of resources, and eager volunteers, they were less likely to get the required amount of consistent physical touch and love. The volunteers needed to tread lightly with the orphans, be warm but not too affectionate, as they would leave at the end of the trip but the children would stay. "I was determined to push through my personal discomfort, to love my neighbor to the best of my God-gifted abilities."

I couldn't hear how Allie spent her days in Jamaica "loving on those sweet, dark faces" again. How she wiped snot from their crusted noses, painted heart murals on their church building walls, and shared Goldfish crackers with the little ones, their bald heads and big dark eyes looking back at her; how she knew her first night there she would be one to bring the gospel to all the nations. With the surf underfoot, back at the resort, she prayed thanks for her new heart of flesh, her compassion for the less fortunate.

I went inside. Allie was building up to tell everyone how she decided to adopt. With her plastic-surgeon husband, they had prayed and sat with their minister and decided to sponsor and foster a pair of sisters, Eva and Ani, originally from Botswana. It was big news, she told our small group, even at her *very* diverse church in the city. When John and I visited for their dedication, church members ogled the girls like zoo animals. They toted them around town as a public declaration of their dedicated love for the church. They even went on local Channel 10 news to talk about their decision to "go multicultural."

"We just don't see color in our family," Allie had said. "The gospel doesn't care what you look like. In Christ there's no race."

At the kitchen counter, I pushed away a tray of pulled pork, opened my computer, and looked up the house where I'd be next week. It looked like a cabin surrounded by woods, red oaks, dogwoods, and magnolias.

Once, at a family weekend in north Georgia in a cabin, Allie told the story of how the girls would video chat their cousins back home and show off their full fridge. "They kept saying how they had never had so much."

When I was with them, the sisters had empty eyes and were always ashy-looking, their skin dry and noses runny, their hair dry and brittle with big gingham bows slapped in. (Allie thought it was okay to wash their hair with plain VO5 only.) A Black church member had tried to encourage Allie to take better care of the girls' hair, even gifted her an edge toothbrush and ecostyler gel. But to hear Allie tell it, the woman had overstepped her bounds, had hurt Allie's feelings and accused her of something much more vile.

"We're doing our best," Allie would tell anyone who'd listen. "We had no idea how much maintenance their upkeep required. That's why I started Mixed Up Mamas, a nonprofit for white parents to learn how to do Black hair."

Online, I dragged the little yellow man on the map down the street to see what was in the area: woods, mostly. It looked quiet. My Google Earth escape was interrupted by a FaceTime call. It was Jodie, my mother-in-law.

"Shauna! Hi, dear! I was hoping to catch you and Allie, my girls." She held her hand to the screen and waved. A David Yurman bangle danced. She'd gifted me a matching one on a vacation last year to 30A. I had no idea where mine was.

"Am I interrupting?"

"We're having small group. Allie is testifying now. I'm just inside, getting refreshments."

Jodie hadn't been happy when Allie adopted the girls. "I'm worried for *them*. It's a big culture shift. They will be teased mercilessly." She'd asked her to reconsider. At dinner earlier in the week, Jodie asked us about how conceiving was going and ordered us calamari to get the "blood going." Then, she prayed over dinner, asking playfully for my womb to be fertilized. I opened my eyes during the prayer to roll my eyes but hers were open, too, and looking into mine. "I hope the baby looks something like me," she had said when we got our entrees. "The best of both worlds—have you seen Megan Markle's kid?—not too dark but not too light. Just right. I'm thinking a button nose and ringlets, you know? She'll be such a cutie. I see her now." But I didn't see her at all.

On the screen, Jodie was talking, but I couldn't really make sense of it.

"They're calling for me outside. I'll tell Allie you checked in."

"I just wanted to say I'm praying."

These people saw my people like hand-me-downs: something you don't expect to last long, something you give away when you're done with it. I hadn't kept a lot of promises to myself in my life, but I swore I'd never bring a child into a family that didn't want her.

The night before I left for my trip, John flipped through a men's health magazine. His eyes moved rapidly over the page, so fast I was convinced he wasn't reading at all. He began mindlessly feather-touching my arm, checking the box for connection, for foreplay, off his list. Allie had been gone for days, but her influence was still here. She'd made herself a hero at small group, and John wanted that for himself. I could feel he wanted to try. He bulged out his boxers. His large tree-trunk runner's legs took up most of the bed. I turned my back to him.

John glanced over and grinned then went back to reading, brows furrowed. His recent corrective veneer appointments gave him a painfully perfect bucky smile. He had a rough go on an ultramarathon trip with his small-group brothers in Utah. He fell face down and knocked out his front teeth. But now, with his movie-star smile, lush, dark hair, black eyes, and doe-like bottom eyelashes, he was undeniably handsome. When we married, I felt like the world was ours. I fought the urge to kick him with my heel.

We said our goodbyes in the driveway, and when I pulled out, I felt light as a balloon. The drive was three hours long and at first, I delighted in the time alone, listening to "Delilah" reruns on the radio, ignoring my phone.

And in the privacy of my car, I did what I'd done for almost a year—when I pulled out of the driveway to my job in the city, as soon as I was out of sight from the house, I reached under my front seat and grabbed my Lo Loestrin Fe I kept inside a mini M&M container. I took them happily every morning on the dot while I cruised to *Morning Edition*. I already cycled through excuses as much as I could: diarrhea, yeast infection, anything to avoid him inside me. He never wanted to have sex when I wasn't ovulating, never when I was on my period, only when I was fertile. I lied about when that was. Faked a longer period by a few days so we were missing our window. Every failed test was an answered prayer and proof that a God somewhere heard me. I knew it was also just the medicine but it felt bigger, felt like the one thing I had. When I swallowed my pills in the morning, I wondered what that month's prospective baby would have looked like. What would having a baby mean for me? All at once I wanted so many things: a daughter, a home, a Volvo, a career. I wanted the marriage of a life-time, companionship, a life partner. I couldn't shake the feeling that the latter was a deception. I saw having some man's child as the ultimate gotcha. I'd have new (some-what chosen) responsibilities, new tethers, new depths of love, and new obligations. In my mind, I was always making a compromise, stretched two places at once.

The music stopped feeling fun. All I could think of was how one version of me was free and empty, the other was full and bound.

The home was tucked in the woods, right off the main road. A yellow farmhouse with faded marigold siding and white trim, imitating the day lillies in the lawn. The white wraparound porch was complete with rockers and a swing. Moths fluttered drunkenly into the sconces. As I parked, I took a look at the patio in front of the carriage house where the preservationist lived. It was messy but he had nice, practical taste. I noted the newish-looking navy hiking boots, the sunproof button-up shirts drying on the banister. He had two fishing poles, a dog bed soaked in dewey debris, and Sierra Nevada bottles rested on their sides.

I stepped over a squeaky bone on my way through the front door. The house was the right amount of anonymity for a guest to feel welcome, filled with the typical *live laugh love* tchotchkes, and there were a few pictures of the owner, a red-headed thin woman and her boyfriend. He was bald and sharply dressed and she held onto his arm with her head on his shoulder, wearing an ecru seersucker dress. I picked up the picture and traced it, studying their faces.

I sat on the couch with my arms tucked in my lap. Then I ran through every room and rolled on every bed like I was in a bad movie. I snooped through the fridge, opened the cupboards, star-fished on my stomach on the living room rug, spreading out until my limbs ached from extension.

In the bathroom, I started the shower. John and I usually did our showers back to back so one of us was at the vanity while the other was stepping into the shower. I took my clothes off and took my hair down. I looked at myself from all angles. Standing on my tip toes, I looked at the shape of my calves. Then I stood straight on, with arms clasped above my head, then from behind. Putting on my shower cap, I took one more glance while the fog filled on the glass.

That night, I got into bed and thought about the first time I took a pregnancy test.

When John and I were both in graduate school in Charleston, living in different parts of town, he would come over and roughly fuck me a few times a week. We were supposed to be waiting for marriage, but we also went to a hip, born-again church where no one seemed to care. Afterwards, we'd eat cold ramen on my living room floor, feeling the breeze from the open windows. With the stress of my graduate program, I had skipped periods before, but this one time I was running close to sixty days late. I didn't drive much unless I was heading into town for class, so I walked down the road to the Dollar General next to Spanky's Wings and the Dominican salon where the smell of singed new growth was so strong my eyes would water. My feet signaled the bing-bong-sounding noise, announcing my presence to the store, where there was a dingy glow. Nothing seemed more humiliating than buying a cheap, behind-the-counter HCG pregnancy test—surely my first time deserved more ceremony— but it was all I could afford. To stall, I went through the aisles, picking up urgent necessities like strawberry soda and generic Fig Newtons. I loaded White Rain body wash in my basket, its goop the color of the Atlantic. When I read the back of the L.A. Looks hair gel container for thirty minutes and could no longer balk, I walked up to the register and asked the woman behind the counter for a test.

"The cheapest one, thanks," I said as she pointed without saying a word to the Plexiglas behind her. I loaded my snacks and soda on the cash wrap and waited for her to ring them. She was striking, with a smooth mahogany face pierced by high cheekbones. She felt about my age, with long Senegalese twists; her fluffy glue-on eyelashes fluttered like Pampas grass. Her acrylics were neat, long, and lacquered with hand-painted flowers, and even though she smiled at me warmly, I couldn't stop looking at the tattoo above her name tag that read *trust no one* in a fountain script below her collar bone. Her hair swished around, moving like black water across her back.

"I'm nervous," I laughed.

"I can tell. I always know who is coming in here for a test. People linger." She smiled. "You ready?" I glanced at her name tag. *Ashanti.*

"Maybe? I just don't want a baby right now, you know?" I sighed, switched my weight on my feet. "I have so much going on. I wouldn't feel good having one when I know I don't want it."

She frowned. "I felt the same way when I had my first one, but you grow to love them. I think a lot of women feel the way we do. But babies are stubborn. When they come, they come, it's like they want to be here. You'll be fine, it'll come natural to you, I feel it."

She waved her hand around me as if in my aura confirmed this.

Ashanti looked like she'd had her baby recently. Her stomach was the only soft-looking thing on her firm body; it squished on the sides, poking out of her company polo. She bagged my things and I felt her eyes on my back as I shuffled out the door.

I decided to take the test the next morning in Byer Hall, in the second-floor bathroom of my main academic building. I parked across from St. Paul's Episcopal, its stained glass glinting in the sun. To get to my 2 p.m. class I had to pass through the ring of fire, a catty-cornered area of crosshair where the red brick abortion clinic sat across from the pink-and-yellow-painted pregnancy resource center. On weekdays, anti-abortion protesters in swollen, white New Balance tennis shoes stood outside with white posters with photos of unborn bodies, bloody quarter-dollar sized ruby blobs with tiny fingers and curled legs. I passed the posters with my head down as if they could smell me out and sense what I was considering.

Once situated inside, I excused myself from class and went to the bathroom and held the test in between my legs. I felt hot piss rinse my palm as I held the piece of plastic and its paper fabric strip in the stream. I placed the test on top of the toilet paper dispenser then set a timer for ten minutes. I sat there with my underwear around my ankles, frozen. I texted John a little. I'd been avoiding him. I said I was fine, just on my period. He texted back "figured :)" When the test turned up negative, I stared at it then shoved it in the wastebasket, feeling relieved and a little sad motherhood hadn't chosen me.

In the morning, I woke up early and piled Folger's into the Mr. Coffee. I looked over the house rules and instructions and planned to take out the trash and put it by the curb later that evening. As I waited for the coffee to brew,

I counted the black octagons in the subway tile. I hadn't had more than a fleeting thought of John or his family since I had woken up, and I loved the feeling of not being tied to him. I decided to meditate, to pray to shake it off. I was happy with what I had. Sitting cross-legged on the kitchen floor, I took a deep breath and thought about what John meant to me. I searched my mind for a vision of the two of us, but it never came.

The window in the kitchen looked out onto the porch then over into an empty plot of land that bottomed into a ravine filled with dense, green kudzu. The summer clover was high, and fat carpenter bees buzzed low to the ground. Down the way, beyond the clearing, was a small red brick house with a slanted roof. A black walnut tree three times its size floated above it, covering the house in a cast of shade. The neighbor below was standing in the yard, looking over into the ravine, then up at the sky. I watched her until she went inside.

The retirement party was in the evening at six p.m. at Vanessa's house on Wednesday. I had errands to run before then. Vanessa wanted a hummingbird cake, lemon icebox pie, cookies, and barbecue. I'd called weeks in advance to place my pick-up orders, but I had to drive into Chattanooga to get everything. It felt a bit simple for my big sister, but I was happy to give her what she wanted. I loved how easy it was to please her, as Vanessa said exactly what she meant to me and to anyone.

Sitting on the porch in my pajamas I listened to the cardinals and sipped another cup of weak Folgers, planning. The preservationist was in his driveway loading his car in wrinkled khakis and a dry-cleaned Brooks Brothers looking shirt. I wondered why he was up so early. I waved goodbye and he waved back.

I had a budget for the week that John and I had agreed on. But after my morning on the porch I had the overwhelming urge to make myself pretty. I spent the afternoon playing dress-up: blow drying my hair, painting my nails, and shaving my legs. I bought a new blouse and push-up bra at Hammer's.

That afternoon, I was sitting in the rocking chair when the neighbor, Neil, walked over to the house to introduce himself. He was close enough to smell, clean like lime leaves and grapefruit. Neil was on a ten-month contract, here to inspect the stained glass at All Saints Chapel and make repair suggestions. His hair was oiled back in pomade dark waves. His eyes were large black saucers. We talked a bit and he offered to show me around, then asked if I was free for a drink that night. I was.

We walked over into Sewanee, and Neil suggested a bar called Shenanigans. The campus looked out of French antiquity, so beautiful I held back tears I didn't expect. Its Gothic architecture loomed, aglow in the evening from the golden street lights. I ran my hands across the sandstone, still warm from the morning sun. The spires of the chapel seemed to pierce through the stars and the stained glass bloomed like a kaleidoscope rose. Church bells rang as the hour turned, reminding me, at least for now, I was here, here, here.

Shenanigans was loud and wet, stuffed with inebriated summer-school students. We walked mostly in silence, afraid of our arms touching. I looked up at Neil many times, trying to figure out what I thought about him. He looked normal-ish, a lot like John. He even carried himself similarly, like such a nice guy, long dark hair, stubble coming through on his chin. I ignored the sick feeling in my stomach and ordered a double gin and pineapple.

"Your neighbor is kind of weird," I said as we looked for a table. "She just stands in that yard and looks into that ravine, then goes inside. Do you know anything about her?"

"Oh Caroline? Yeah, she just moved here from California, works for Patagonia. She calls herself a big idea person. Said she was obsessed with Daniel Boone since she was a kid, wants to make space for a new definition of the South."

I rolled my eyes. I sat at a table in the corner. Instead of sitting across from me, he slid onto the bench beside me.

"She has some nerve, but she's determined. She has some rich granddaddy who owns a summer home up in Dandridge so she calls herself half Appalachian. Everytime she speaks I want to remind her technically we live in the Cumberland plateau. She bought the house sight unseen when she saw it on Zillow, sold her part time textile company, and drove out here. She keeps passing out flyers, fundraising to fill that ravine up and open a community garden."

"Oh."

Neil took my hand, turned it over in his and stroked up and down my inner wrist. He put his other hand around my shoulder and pulled me closer, leaning into my hair. His breath stank like a stale cigar; his voice sounded like a fly in my ear.

"Everybody new here is doing that, it seems. I've been researching the trend, actually. I published a paper on it last month. They are obsessed with Pinterest and van life and come from over there and move here and then lose their shit and leave. She won't last more than a year."

Before the drinks came he was running his knuckle around the hem of my shorts on the side of my thigh. He wore a signet ring on his pinky that felt cold against my skin. I didn't tell him to stop. I didn't tell him I thought it was presumptuous or that it sent lightning through me either. I let him touch me. We talked about his research, where we went to college, and his hopes for partner at his firm. Neil didn't ask me any questions about myself. I kept smiling, nodding, gulping.

"The sad thing is what she doesn't know. Miss Caroline from California, she thinks she knows what she's in for. Summer is lying to her. That roof she thinks she owns is cheap tin and when those walnuts drop later this fall it will be miserable for months. The noise will be painfully loud, four times what you think it would be, and cause so much damage it will be too expensive to replace. She can't fill that ravine up, there's too much shade, she won't grow a thing. She's so proud because she thinks she figured it out, but it will be awful for her. It really will. But I'm not here long. And I don't care enough to tell her."

After the third mixed drink and a split plate of fried pickles, I was practically in his lap. My husband hadn't texted me all day. He was abiding the boundary we set before I left. I was only out with a new friend, I told myself. We stayed until last call.

Walking back buzzed from the bar, I took in the rush of scenery: the full, full trees, wide sky, winding road and river. He was holding my hand now, and I took my shoes off. It was a hot night but not too damp in the air. The soles of my feet slightly burned. As we approached the porch I could feel the question between us. I ran my hands through his hair and got caught on the ends beginning to curl up. Embarrassed, I went ahead of him coolly, walking toward the door on my side.

"I have a few bottles of wine if you want to hang some more."

"Sure. I just need a minute to get myself together. You can let yourself in? Give me five minutes?" He nodded and I caught him looking at my body.

Running the shower would be too obvious, I thought, so I ran the faucet and stripped. I ripped my underwear off and stuffed them into the hamper, then pressed myself into the sink and rinsed off the sweat from hours outside drinking liquor and rubbing against one another. I wasn't sure what to do when I met him at the edge of the couch. We hugged gently until I suggested we sit. I played some music from my phone and got up to get some glasses from the kitchen. The wine looked expensive; it was natural, which excited me. John only bought Two-Buck Chuck from Trader Joes. We drank glass after glass and talked.

After a bout of awkward silence, he found the side of my thigh again and started rubbing. His confidence felt practiced. I ran my hands up and down his arms and his legs, smoothing the coarseness of his leg hair and wishing to feel that pressed against me. The way that he touched me was rough yet needy, and I liked this. My husband never touched me right anymore. I could feel the formula he worked through in his brain: *touch here, kiss here, rub here.* John was a words guy, overinflating compliments that he thought women would like to hear. When he touched me I felt as dry as the Mojave.

Eventually the two of us were in our underwear. I dripped through mine. Knuckle grazes turned into shy grabs around my hips, then full palms of my dimpled ass as he pulled at the tender and browned flesh of my inner thighs.

In between kissing, I let it slip that I was married, and Neil mentioned he technically was, too. "We're separated," he said as he kissed my neck. "I've got one kid. Simon. They live in Memphis." I wished he'd shut up. As he pulled my shirt above me, my bones melted. A warm, wetness filled me. Blood rushed to my head. Neil grabbed all the soft round parts of me, then took his left hand and ran it down the center of my body, opening me with two fingers. I was surprised at my own slickness; the bulb of myself felt milky and ripe.

As he worked inside me, I began to dry up. I pushed my hips against him, helping him find the place that felt best for me. Moving my hand on top of his, I made tiny counter clockwise circles, trying to show him how to get me there, but he swatted me away. "Relax, let me take control." He grinned. Closing my eyes, I remembered how much validation John needed when we were intimate. He liked sucking on my earlobe. After sex, he'd ask me to put my legs up on the wall for twenty minutes so his sperm would stick. After that, he needed space. He got up, showered, and ran to Weigels to get Big Gulp or a Klondike Bar. He texted me from the gas station.

How was it? 1 to 10?

Incredible babe, I'd say. *Beyond any number I could give.*

I pulled Neil's hand out of me. "I can't handle it anymore."

"I figured you'd like that," he said, then licked his fingers. I sat up and pulled my clothes on and went to sit on the porch. He said he'd be with me soon. Said he needed a minute and winked. I closed the door behind me.

The heat off our bodies swirled as we sat side by side on the rocking swing. Neil started kneading at the spot on the nape of my neck, giving me a crick. Light inside the little brick house down the way turned on.

It wasn't *terrible*. We'd been drinking, it was only

our first time together. Everyone's nervous their first time. I imagined a passionate re-do where I felt actual pleasure. Our new life played in my mind. We stayed here. I worked remotely. We bought a two-bedroom, one-bathroom house on the Domain. His contract extended. I kept the house clean. I became a stepmother to his white, blond, blue-eyed son. *It's the same, but different,* I told myself. Neil was on his phone now, texting someone.

"I had a great time." I moved my hand across his lap, played with his zipper. "Come back tomorrow?" He moved my hand back.

"Unfortunately, I don't think I can. Melissa is coming with Simon for the weekend. I leave here pretty soon anyway. Summer's almost over. I think it's better if this is it."

I curled my lips up and felt sick. "Are you okay?" Neil asked. My head swam. I ran down the front steps as my gin adventure turned sour in my stomach.

"Let me know if you need anything! I'm going to check on the dog," Neil hollered as a goodbye as I threw up in the grass.

On my way to my sister's the next evening, I thought about how stupid I was. Hours later, after he left, I'd roamed the front yard like a stray, getting the courage to knock on his front door, and stood in front of his house in my Snoopy pajamas and silk bonnet, only to run back to my side when his dog barked and a light turned on. In the afternoon, as I backed out of the driveway, headed to run the final errands before my sister's party, Melissa and Simon pulled up in a white Range Rover. Neil walked to his "ex" and tongue-kissed her deeply. Simon jumped up and down. "Daddy! Daddy!"

The retirement party, though, was a success. Vanessa's co-workers pitched in and gave her a down payment for an RV. I avoided her all evening, wanting her to have her fun. I cleaned and restocked like a bag girl at Whole Foods. My sister wore a gold jumpsuit from a thrift store, and her whole community—ranging from twenty-somethings to folks well into late life—came out to support her.

As I cleared the trash, I took the bags to the curb and sat on the sidewalk, listening to the music thump behind me. I looked for the moon. "There you are." My sister came outside and found me, offering me a cigarette.

"John says smoking decreases my chances of getting pregnant," I said, taking one.

"I don't give a shit what John says. This is *my* night." Vanessa had the best laugh. She put her arm around my waist, kissed my cheek. "Thanks for all this. You coming over or what?"

At her kitchen table, my sister made us breakfast for a midnight snack: Sister Schubert's rolls and butter-fried Wamplers sausage with hot chocolate mix drowned in hot, frothy whole milk. At the table, we said grace and tore into the food, enjoying the salty pork on the soft pillows of dough. I was more sheepish than my usual self, looking out the window. I remembered I had bite marks all on my neck like I was fourteen. While we ate our food, I made small talk, asked my sister where she was going to go first in the RV. "Utah? Maybe Wyoming? Have you been to the Tetons yet? Heard it's incredible." Her eyes burned a hole through me.

"You fucked that asshole neighbor? Wow."

"I wouldn't call it *that* necessarily." I squeezed my knees together, my insides ached.

"What are you doing, Shauna? What's going on with you?"

"Maybe don't shame me?" I took another bite. "I'm trying, I really am."

"I haven't seen you all week. When we talk, all I hear is about the people in your little church group. How are *you?*"

I dipped the side of my biscuit into a shallow green bowl of apple butter, took a bite, and chewed until my jaw hurt.

"I'm fine." I knew how Vanessa felt about John, about Allie, about all of them. When I'd first started spending time with them, she was confused, then angry—at my parents for taking me to their church, at me for not understanding how they saw us.

She stared at me, waiting. "Well, was it at least good?" she asked, mouth full.

I bugged my eyes at her. "Sis, let's not even go there." I looked away. She laughed and put her hand over her mouth. I felt like a fool.

"Shauna, I don't care what you do. But I want you to be happy. And honest. You're worth more than this, deserve better than this—than a family who's more or less breeding you or treating you like some jungle fever fling. None of these white people can save you. And they surely can't give you what you need."

"Come on, Vanessa."

"No 'come on.' You are my smart, beautiful baby sister, Shauna. You're a grown woman now. You've got to make these decisions on your own. How long do you want to live these lies? Aren't you sick and tired of it? Don't you want more?"

My last day in the little house in the woods, John sent me a text saying he was counting down the days until he saw me. He was upset with Allie. She was pregnant, and she'd announced on Facebook that she'd be naming the child—boy or girl—after their father. John wanted his child to be the third. I lied and told him I was sorry. Mary-Martha was hosting Taco Tuesday. We had to bring margarita mix. He wanted me to send an ETA from my GPS as soon as I got in the car.

It was close to three in the morning, and in a few hours I'd be on my way back home.

Out on the porch, I looked at that big walnut tree in the moonlight and thought about what Neil had said, about this fall the walnuts would ruin the woman's vision of the quaint life. What did he know of what she wanted for her life?

Dawn broke before me, and the world rose to meet it: blue to yellow to orange. I had a headache. I rubbed my jaw. The clock in me was ticking down, ringing—getting closer to the end of my time. John was waiting for me, but I wasn't going home.

I texted Vanessa.

That RV going to have room for two? ✳

THE BEST YEARS OF YOUR LIFE

Our campus opened in the former two-story Sears at West Town Mall. Take the escalator up to find me. From my office window, I see the other side of the vacant department store. Leggy mannequins with missing heads and balloon breasts line the carpet. Dusty signs in faded red scream LIQUIDATION SALE: EVERYTHING MUST GO.

New Life University has chains in almost every US state, in most cities with a population of over 90,000 residents. Four years here and they'll be changemakers. I let potential students know I believe in them in my admissions office, blubbering platitudes on my headset, my desk a crumbling corner of Ollie's Bargain Outlet Formica. I lie from 8 a.m. to 4:30 p.m.

Prospectives come in all the time with bright eyes, saying they got a sign, a hunch, a prodding to come and finish what they started. That sign is nothing more than cache cookies tracking their 1 a.m. Googles: "how to start over" or "how to go back to school with a 1.9 gpa." Here, people can pay $30,000 a semester to get a PhD in Leadership—universities like mine are for-profit cash cows. Read the fine print: We're not accredited. These grades don't exist. No one takes them seriously, no matter the transcript, no matter the hard work. We advertise ourselves as a selective institution, so people think I saw something special in them when they get their acceptance letter in the mail signed personally by *Yours Truly*. But that means nothing. We aren't selective because we accept 99 percent of applications. Most I forget, but some I remember.

I keep thinking how I worked for months on a weathered grandmother with peach-pallor skin and Pentecostal length hair. After driving all the way from Oneida, she told me her plan of graduating here, then law school, so she can defend her grandson, who was wrongly accused of assisted homicide. Police had been watching his activity on the dark web for a while, she said. He got caught up on buying PCP through the mail. They'd discovered some semi-automatic weapons in his home, too. He'd been on these forums reading manifestos. That's how they found him, tracked his IP address and everything. "He spent all day on that damn internet," she mentioned in passing. "He's locked up and it's so unfair. He's my baby." I didn't totally understand what all he'd done or if she understood it. She had the plan piped out all on a piece of white computer paper. Her T-shirt read WORLD'S BEST MEEMAW and a Tweety bird keychain held her house keys on a carabiner. It hooked in a loop on her White Stag jeans.

Our team in the office is five strong. Our VP of enrollment and assistant director are out most days, either commuting to Nashville headquarters or stepping out for a business "lunch" from 10:30 a.m. to 3 p.m. at Nama. That usually leaves me, Gena, and Mahogany to manage the students and rake in deposits. Mahogany is fine, just has a nervous laugh that feels clinical. I don't talk much to Gena, though. She takes the job too seriously, is so severe with her students, and never regulates herself. She always freaks the hell out and smooths her slacks down with her moist palms. She talks like a mouse, too. Once I slapped a Post-it on her chair that said *SPEAK UP* but she'd walked in on me doing it and we just stared at each other. At the team mixer last month, she blacked out on Hypnotiq at TGI Fridays. I held her hair back while she got sick in the big stall. Once, when she didn't pass an internal CRM competency exam, she threw her whole chicken parmesan from Gondolier on the conference room wall. The stain stuck there for weeks.

My apartment complex, The Center, sends out emails for domestic violence hotlines. There's an incentive if people report, then a link to CDC data around physical abuse. The picture on the hotline is insensitive: a brunette with a photoshopped galaxy bruise on her eye looking sullenly at the camera. The property manager left a voice-mail on my phone about a survey they were taking after people in the complex complained about disturbances. They think someone is hurting me or I'm hurting some-one else, but I live alone. I buy ten plates at a time at Goodwill—Chinoiserie, crystal, porcelain, Corning—and throw them on the linoleum floor before my work day at the "college." I get so sad cause I lie to people every day to pay my bills. Really, I pay *some* of my bills: I pay the rent with my lousy salary and my parents write a check for my utilities and groceries. But it's gotten worse since my boo Caden said he wanted to see other people. The three folks on my floor either don't notice or they are too afraid to say something. They don't check in, they don't say hello—just put their keys in their doors quickly, pressing in with their thighs or whole bodies to avoid small talk.

Most mornings, I cry on the way to work, flicking off people who have the nerve to drive slower than I want. Most mornings, it rains here. My car is slick, slicing through the pavement while I blast heat at my feet. Most mornings, I wear a blazer from JCPenney that needs to be washed. Most mornings, I don't even let myself think of where I'd rather be.

Two weeks ago, Caden, my sorta-boyfriend, beat me to it and dumped me at Red Lobster. I think about it on my breaks from work. I walk over to the Sears side and I lay on the closeout Sealy mattresses—only three are left—while I stare at the popcorn ceiling. If I prop up on my side, I can see the Smokies from the window. I've got a feeling the manager, Daryl, hates when I come up here—he's always looking at me like *there* she *is again*. He got really mad when, after I fell asleep, I spilled a bean burrito on a $2,000 pillow-top Beautyrest. I wanted to be the one to break up first, but I was always the more attached. Caden is a shift manager at J.Crew and wants to be a journalist. He walks hard to hear himself clack across the floor in his Men's Warehouse loafers. His Accutane-fresh skin looks like a newborn, except for the moony craters lining his cheeks.

"I was supposed to be in *The New York Times* by now," he said when I dropped by the store on a dead weekday last month. He had his hair cut in a sailor crew style, dyed jet black with Revlon Colorsilk for $2.69 a box. I used to dye his shoulder-length hair honey auburn and wash it out as he leaned over his kitchen sink. His apartment in the JFG building with the shining coffee logo is a dump, except for the black-and-white busboy tile on the kitchen floor. I liked to look at it and imagine I was in Paris. He'd been reading a lot of Eckhart Tolle lately at Barnes and Noble, meaning he just held the book and read for twenty minutes in the store, then put it back before he left. I kept telling him about the grandmother who's been coming by. How I don't feel right about it. I found myself thinking about her when I woke up. We'd started chatting on the phone for hours sometimes. I liked talking to her. "You think I can really do it?" she'd ask me.

He told me I was "trauma dumping" on him. But what is a relationship for if I can't talk about what's in *my* life? So we haven't talked since then. I've been working overtime, first in and last out, to take my mind off losing him. I visualize being "preoccupied." I keep remembering what he said about me: *energy vampire, toxic, self indulgent.* He said I virtue signal. I'm all talk and no action. I whine about others but don't make anything better. "Anyone can complain," he said. "But you still take your paycheck every month, don't you?"

I've got a bang situation at the moment. I'm so sad I can barely wash my hair. Last time I was in a funk this bad, I read in *Essence* that embracing my God-given curl pattern could foster self-trust, so about seven years ago I quit the relaxer and shaved off my nipple-length, colonized tresses. But I'm too lazy to take care of it right, too impatient to get the L(otion) O(il) C(ream) method down, too frustrated to detangle tip to root, so I do a lot of puffy flat braids.

These days, the back of my hair is dog fur–matted. For the past month, I've been pulling my honeycomb-wad of hair into an elegant French twist: gripping the hair in a Goody rubber band, slicking down what I can with Ecostyler gel, then using a tortoise shell banana clip. Cute!

Since I'm a natural sis-tah now, the back of my head has coiled so tight I can't get my hands through it. Which leads me to sink, wash my "curtain" bangs, blow dry, then flatiron them a few times a week for some professional, face-framing movement. Caden once said I looked like a pageboy.

Even though I hate this job, I try to be inspiring, helpful—a model minority. I want my boss to praise me, say I'm good at what I do. On my desk I have my computer, some pens, a Bath and Body Works Mahogany Teakwood candle, and some Kenyan textiles from my year abroad. I have an elevator pitch for our open house events. I tell students about the places education can take you. The PowerPoint presentation is a rip off of *Oh, the Places You'll Go!*. Prospective students drink weak coffee with powdered creamer out of Styrofoam cups and smell like the cigarette they smoked nervously on the way in, while I talk to them about the power of innovation.

I show pictures of places "alumni" have traveled to after their graduation. People love the segment about a former business student, Ron, and his blow-up-doll wife, who run a modeling startup in Ecuador. They ooh and ah over the pictures of him in Quito. They stare at the city's gilded, Jesuit cathedral, *la Compañía*, where the walls drip in real sixteenth-century baroque gold. They want to see the Spanish influences in the old city fused with the indigenous, shown through blotches of bright colors, yellow, pink, blue, and red—splashed against humble cottage houses stacked in layers through the hills. Go here, you can get there, you can go anywhere.

The woman who thinks she can free her grandson from prison has weekly meetings scheduled with me. I signed an NDA when I took the job here agreeing to only speak of the college positively! The average student will accumulate $90,000 in private student loans, but I can't say that. The woman sits and shares with me about her grandson as a boy—her first grandbaby, the sensitive one. He's up at Bledsoe County Correctional. She tells me when she drives over to Pikeville and visits, they split a bag of Cool Ranch Doritos. Last time, he looked less motivated. "I'm getting you OUT of here baby," she said. "Chin up." He shrugged. "It's not so bad, Grandma. And what's better back home? What's even waiting for me?" She brings me brochures of places where she wants to study law. Last month it was William and Mary. Last week, Pepperdine by the water. She's one of those people who's never gone west of the Mississippi. She hasn't turned in an application yet, but she wants to go over her ten-year plan. Again, and again, and again.

"You can't manage what you don't measure. You have to see it to become it."

She writes down her plan, point A to point Z, on another sheet of computer paper, marking it with a fat red Expo marker.

It's February, so I have my space heater going. My ankle skin is cracking. When the grandmother finally turns in her application, it contains her admissions essay about the power of possibility. It's full of run-on sentences, but the flow is nice. I sit in my office with my legs up on my desk, reading through her words. She took time to write this carefully. We didn't require an admissions essay, but she wanted me to know her, to see the effort. The following week when she comes by for our meeting, I hand her the acceptance package, and she leaps across the desk and holds me. She has me stand up and read it out loud to her.

"You're a good woman," she tells me, as she squeezes tighter. "Your kindness is changing us, we won't forget it."

I don't know what to say to that.

The grandmother asks if she can take me out to dinner for being such a great help on her journey. It's close to the end of the day, so I clock out. Gena is working late, so I walk past without saying goodbye. To freshen up, I spray some Calgon Take Me Away I found in the women's restroom on my neck. We walk over to Shoney's, our bodies close together for warmth, the breath from our noses in sync, circling above us. Tonight her T-shirt reads, "Let Go, Let God." At the crosswalk, she says the shortcake is to die for.

I haven't been to Shoney's since I was a little girl. I remember how the bacon sat in its golden grease. Once my brother and I saw a man pile his plate high of hot, powdered eggs drenched in orange government-cheese sauce. My father said he was smart to get his money's worth.

When we walk in, she is close to me, shoulder to shoulder. She puts her hand on my back, scratches my spine up and down a little. And after we get seated, she has me go first. Tells me to get whatever I want. ✳

COLLEEN

olleen was always beyond me, a full handful out of my reach. Her bedroom was nautical-themed. As if the room itself was the interior of a shoddy submarine, her stepmother, Dorinda, painted portholes on the walls as a new mommy consolation. Those windows took you somewhere else. Through them you could visit a small, blue place with scenes of kelp forests, brackish water, mangroves, or coral. With a hand-crank boom box covered in 3-D whale stickers, Colleen liked to play "Pachelbel With Ocean" sounds for me. "Close your eyes and really feel this one," she'd say. Having only visited Myrtle Beach once as a young girl, the waves made a permanent impression on her.

Colleen lived in Westerwood on the historic registry, fifteen minutes from me on the south side. Her cul-de-sac was owned by the Advenist church so like-minded folks could commune together. Their house was a Dutch Colonial, Mr. Clyde liked to remind us, with sparkling white-gable ends, plush ivy, and a genuine wood-powered furnace.

When Clyde Witherspoon left his first wife for the second, the family had to leave their congregation in Germantown. They were reassigned permanently to First Church of Farragut, where he was able to keep in service as an usher. That's where we met, the only grade-school girls in the sanctuary that Sabbath.

That first summer, Colleen's legs were too long for the twin bed frame. When we lay side by side, looking out those ports, half her calf flopped over the edge and her toes almost skimmed the floor. She'd been wearing something from her new box of hand-me-downs. Her recent favorite was a T-shirt that said *COOL* with a penguin floating on an ice cube. Ever practical, Colleen paired it with smooth khaki pedal pushers and Tevas she was growing into.

As the seasons changed, winter put me and Colleen to work splitting logs for the fire. In her Patagonia puffer coat, a size too small, she'd hold the ax while I steadied the log. Raising her arms over her head, face red as fresh blood, I noticed the stitching ripping in the armpit of her child-sized jacket. She'd bring the blade down and crack the wood and the echo ran through every street in the neighborhood. The sound moving through us, we'd howl and cut the wood of another, then another. The same pair of crows often flew above us, stirred at the noise. One time, while Colleen yelled, her cheeks gripped and I saw the baby blue bands around her braces and the buds of her wisdom teeth peaking on the back of her jaw. Her father held a bake sale in the neighborhood to get those teeth fixed. Dorinda wore a pleather mini skirt with a rhinestone belt. The whole church showed up. Colleen looked like she was drowning while we stood outside and goaded our goodies. Back then her crowded crossbite went in seven directions. Mr. Clyde had her smile real big at everyone so they could see how badly she needed to be fixed.

We had to roll the wood back to the house in an Ace Hardware wheelbarrow, our fingers numb. Colleen's cheeks usually turned ruddy while mine stayed brown. Mr. Clyde met us at the door out back then brought us inside, palming our bicep muscles, calling us "his budding feminists."

The Witherspoons didn't have a TV or a radio as the devil could get in your brain through the waves. So, on the Sabbath we played board games or read Amish romance stories. By the fire, Colleen would work a dolphin puzzle on her stomach. And I'd rest by her feet, reading about some young woman off in Pennsylvania, painfully shy, anticipating her wedding night.

Often we ate dinner by candlelight. The Witherspoons said the power went out daily—"*A home built in the*

1700s was not meant to support modern appliances"—
and because of their commitment to preservation,
they didn't dare change the wiring. We could learn to
be comfortable with discomfort. But the stack of bills
Colleen and I went through in the bottom bathroom
cabinet said otherwise.

I liked to stay over for Sabbath family dinner after
service. My own family took the resting thing too seriously and would nap and fast until the next morning.
It was either my baby bed in our cramped house or
Colleen's, so I chose her.

We usually ate veggie roast, Big Franks, and potatoes or Shepherd's pie, lukewarm. Colleen sometimes
brushed her hand against my thigh, signaling me to look
at Dorinda in her boatneck blouse. The both of us antic-
ipated starting our periods soon, which induced a joint
obsession with every feminine body around us. I was flat-
chested with puffy nipples, while Colleen's breasts were
already heavy and round. Convinced Dorinda had sili-
cone implants, something about the candlelight made her
look even more bulbous. The veins in her "girls," as Mr.
Clyde called them, glowed orange under soft light.

If the fire went out at night, we went to the yard to
cut more wood. Mr. Clyde said it built character while
he stuffed sea-shell hazelnut bon-bons in his impossibly
small mouth. With two headlamps on and galoshes, we
trudged out back and wandered, looking for places to
gather and split.

Past the house and the clearing, it was as dark as

the Midnight Zone. Navigating with intuition, Colleen would find our spot, pick some lumber, and get to it, hogging the responsibility. Driving the wedge against the wood she would cut and cut and cut, the *pank* noise clapping off the night sky. Colleen looked like a large, frustrated baby in her clothes, in her highwaters with socks up her calf, toes clearly stuffed in her galoshes. Half of her forearm stuck out her bright yellow jacket. Her chest looked like it would burst from the zipper. I waited for the teeth to give.

Looking back up the field, Advent candles lit the windows of the Dutch Colonial while Mr. Clyde stood there, as a silhouette looking down at us. Dorinda crocheted a blanket by the fireplace in a halter top. With the white pillar candles and fir Christmas garland in every window, the house looked smack dab out of a Thomas Kinkade painting, except the panes were rotting, and Mr. Clyde had run out of paint to finish the house—the front was robin egg blue while the back and sides stayed a dusty brown. He passed along a firm thumbs up as a consolation. It was pitch black and starting to drizzle. Still, we hadn't filled the wheelbarrow.

"How did your dad meet Dorinda?"

Colleen chopped more. She was silent, muttering to herself about what I asked her and slamming that wedge into another.

"I'm not sure."

"Where's your real mom?"

"Somewhere else. I don't really want to talk about it."

"Okay."

I wiped rain from my face and waited for her to ask about me. She kept chopping.

In the light from my headlamp, Collen looked slick with oil. Her mouth was bass-like—wide open—and her lips rested on the edge of her middle brackets. The fatty middle part of her upper lip got caught on the metal and ripped a little. A drop of blood hung there. She kept going and the noise kept pushing, reverbing: *pank*, *pank*, *pank*.

On one large log, she brought the top of her ax above her head and the inseam under her baby-looking coat arm busted all the way. Down feathers floated around us.

I stepped in for her and steadied the last log. Instead, she put me in my place and came down on it harder than necessary. She wiped her mouth, muttered, "Sorry." She barely missed my fingers. ✳

BITCH BABY

Nobody talks about it really. I drove to the hospital with blood on my good clothes. I couldn't wipe it up fast enough. I felt it dry and gel brown in my hands. I tried to help Reggie keep his head upright, so he wouldn't choke to death. I did the best I could—I didn't know yet. I couldn't keep him from staining the seats of Mama's car.

At the hospital, it took a while for anyone to care. They packed the gash on his skull (the one on his forehead too) to stop the bleeding while he screamed on the gurney, floating in and out. They thought he sounded hysterical. I heard them say so, "hysterical," as he said over and over again that he couldn't see. Mama made it there and rocked over him and prayed the best she could, even though she knew why Reggie was going down to Savannah in the first place, to do those sweet things.

I know she would never say it, but Mama felt it happened because of his sin.

"We are the company we keep," she reminded us all the time, giving a penny if we could recite the Proverb right. *He who walks with the wise grows wise, but a companion of fools suffers harm.* "What happens to you is a result of what you've done, who you really are, who you know. What you do when no one's watching."

She'd say this, in some version, every which way we went: in the pews before service, in the kitchen with sweat beads on her forehead, biting her nails to the quick as we waded through the aisles of Piggly Wiggly.

Who are you? said Mama in my head. *Who am I?* I wondered. When we were little, she worked a lot and couldn't always watch us, but somehow, Mama always felt present, and so did God—both watching us deeply, both knowing who we really were in the heart.

It wasn't too hard keeping Reggie's secret, mostly because there wasn't one to keep.

Reggie switched too much and smacked his gum too loud and looked in the mirror too long. People knew before he did. I remember how I found him once in Mama's bathroom shirtless and rubbing red lipstick on his full mouth. Chet Baker was on the radio and the room smelled of cigarettes and gardenias, and I watched him from the door frame because he was beautiful and his lips were full enough to carry the color well. I loved the way Reggie watched himself and caught his body moving; the slick, taut lines of his chest and shoulders, the grace of him, the full moon of his face.

In the evenings, Reggie and I would lay on the floor of my bedroom while we flipped through copies of *Southern Woman* and *Vogue* we stole from Claudine's house. Saffron and mustard-colored modern kitchens filled the pages. Reggie liked open floor plans with plain backsplashes. I dreamed of flowing patterns and big windows.

"Celine, just so you know, when I move over there I'm gonna marry the doctor and our house will look just like this." Reggie flipped through the glossy pictures of craftsman houses. I looked around his bedroom walls, which he'd plastered with cuttings from magazines like this. I stayed quiet for a bit.

"What about Jeb Matthews? I asked. "He was nice wasn't he? Whatever happened with him?"

Reggie sucked in his teeth.

"He's a nobody, Ceiley, I want to be with somebody. I'm trying to go somewhere."

Reggie kept flipping and bit on his fingernails.

"What about Donnie Rogers? Y'all went steady for a while, I swear I even think Mama liked him."

He smirked at me and we giggled. "Donnie was sweet

but so plain," Reggie said. "Watching paint dry was more interesting than talking to him."

I got up and walked around.

"There's nothing good coming out of this, Reg. He's married. He don't care about you. Don't be a plaything."

"I know what I want, and it's not here on the island. I have a feeling about our future. We could really do it. There's so much out there waiting for me. Just be happy for me. Please be happy."

I wanted to ask him if he would have a room for me, but mostly I just listened to him and wondered if he would make it out there apart from me in the big waiting world. We'd heard the stories all our lives: about old Jeff Patton and his lovers, Mr. John Gilbertson's thirty-year roommate, and fast Lacey McArthur's harem of women. Would Reggie love it or end up like all the others: stripped naked, black and blue, and hung from a tree?

I held up a picture of a man in his country kitchen: a peach pie on the counter, a shaggy dog at his feet.

"Is this what's waiting out there?" I asked. Reggie rolled his eyes.

For him, I made myself happy, happy, happy.

When we cleaned at Claudine Boatright's, sometimes she didn't really hate us so bad. A plump tobacco heiress with white hair and cloudy sea-glass eyes, her wood and concrete estate sat right off the water on St. Simons Island.

In her right mind, we were barely above her damn dachshunds; she often called us by their names. But sometimes her fading memory made her sweeter. On good days, she considered kindness a Christian duty. There would be snacks out for us in the kitchen with a Bible verse—*Blessed are the meek, for they shall inherit the earth*—and a slice or two of chocolate chess pie atop paper plates, never the good jadeite china. If we wanted water, we would have to grab some from the spigot out back, but Claudine was sure to put plasticware out for us.

When Claudine was out at her bridge games, me and Reggie played with her things, smothering ourselves in her bath oils, sprays of Chanel No. 5, and long strings of her Japanese pearls. We pranced around the foyer and watched ourselves in the windows, taking turns coming down the staircase.

Claudine's daughter Mabel was odd-looking and cruel. Tall and fragile, with severe dark eyes, her prominent Adam's apple bobbed when she swallowed. Mabel considered it better for us to be separate from the people we served. She often pulled her mother to the side, reminding her to only let us use the outhouse at the edge of the estate.

"Don't feel sorry for them, Mother, they can walk. They're built for hard work."

Mabel wanted us to steal, so she set us up often. Something was always a tick off: the silver double-polished and close to the door, an emerald ring left on the sink, $100 casually splayed out across the bedspread, the same pearls we played with dangling off the bed post. But we never took the bait. We just wanted to pretend.

In the summer we often slept over at Claudine's house to watch her things and her grandbabies—Mabel's daughters, who were Irish twins. Harriet and her sister, Debbie, were loose things, both with grown-women breasts at sixteen and green, sad eyes—just enough woman to get them in trouble.

Claudine and Mabel left for the Tennessee mountains in the summer, and her granddaughters were going wild. Older boys came to pick them up after me and Reggie did their make-up and curled their tresses. Our brushes glided through their cornsilk hair, each pass pulling the sweet smell of their shampoo through the room. When we finished dolling them up, we walked the girls out to the cars waiting for them. As soon as they left the driveway, the girls pulled out bottles of apple schnapps.

We watched them wave goodbye until they were a blip in our sight.

When they made it home, which they always did, we would mend them. We combed back their dampened hair and walked them to the bathroom, fanning their pink faces as they spewed syrup-sour vomit in between sobs. But what else was there to do? There was no sense in warning them. White women will do anything when they wanna be in love.

Sometimes when the girls were passed out drunk back at the house, we would help lay them in their beds, then take the money out of their pocketbooks and save it for our weekend trips down to Savannah.

"For our babysitting fee," Reggie would say while he smiled, flashing his canines, counting our cash.

The tips of the enamel were still little from the first years of his life. His front baby teeth never fell out. When the weekend came back around and Claudine drove back up to the house, the sisters would be all smiles, back in their pure goodness. They would have us clean their plates—"Can you put these in the sink?"—and when we took them up, they wouldn't look us in the eye.

But the money was good and the time together was better, and Reggie needed the job to keep up.

He was in love with Dr. Johnson in town. Dr. Johnson liked for Reggie to dress up in women's clothes, padded bra and everything, and meet him outside Pinkie's downtown. It's not that he wanted to be a woman, he would tell me, but he just liked looking like one sometimes. Reggie liked to spend the cleaning money on big tubes of Elizabeth Arden lipstick. He liked the feeling of velvet all over his lips and how the doctor seemed to really need him.

As if he was really something special. Someone worth looking at.

We had big plans that night. While we cleaned the floorboards with old rags and lye, we watched the clock in the living room for 8 p.m. It was hot and sticky, late July, when we left Claudine's. A cousin had come for the girls to take them to Tennessee for the weekend. I told Reggie I'd pick him up after I got ready and grabbed the reefer I kept under my bed.

I'd borrowed Mama's car. She didn't like us to use it after work, but if we begged her she'd give in. Often I met up with Victor when we went to Savannah. He was a nice enough guy with lovesick eyes who was in the service and always bought me Budweiser. We liked to smoke in his car and dance against each other at the bar, while Reggie went off with his lover.

At the house, I rushed in to get my things, hoping to slip past her. Mama was a night person, perpetually restless, walking back and forth, pacing around her twin-sized bed over nothing and everything all the time. Her room sat at the very back of the house. I lingered in the hallway beside my door for a moment and held my breath. She sat in her bedroom in her chair with the windows open. Her feet were up and she was lotioning them. I heard the faint sound of the radio, the Dodgers playing the Braves.

I went into my room and pulled on my nice tight black dress and reached under my bed in the wooden box where I kept all the things I shouldn't. I clipped my hair up high on my head and sprayed Shalimar perfume on my wrist, neck, and between my thighs. I tried to hurry—to slip out and say nothing—but right as I was stepping into the hallway, I heard her clear her throat.

"I need the car, Mama. I'll be back later. I left something at Claudine's."

She didn't say anything. I waited a while.

"Okay, love."

I heard sadness in her voice.

"Reggie and I will get home fine, okay?"

She let out a sigh. "I know you will, Celine. It's an awful world out there. I am glad you got him looking out for you."

Earlier at Claudine's, Reggie had pulled me aside and showed me a new dress he stuffed down in his cleaning bag. He bought the dress from the consignment store. It was silver and beaded and shimmered at the bottom. He glowed as he laid it across his torso and bounced around. I hadn't seen him like this in a while. I told him I would pick him up at the street light around nine that evening, and then we would be off to Pinkie's.

The doctor pumped his head full of European dreams. He told Reggie about France and how people like them could freely live together there. Reggie swore one day they'd move. The doctor would leave his wife and newborn, and Reggie would leave me, and they would start over together.

When I picked up Reggie he was feeling bold. Under his jacket he was already wearing that magnificent dress. It glittered all over him. His hair was fresh with a perm and slicked over to the side, and he was full-grinning; the tips of his teeth showed. I put the car in park and gestured for us to change seats. "You drive," I teased. We got out, meeting one another in the headlights' beam. I grabbed his hand and spun him around in the moonlight as we switched sides.

Reggie took the driver's seat and put the windows down, and I hopped in on the passenger side and started rolling. I lit the papers and made the car glow red. I passed him the blunt. I put my hand out the window and felt the air slip between my fingers. It was going fine until the cop car pulled behind us.

"Fucking pigs," he sighed.

Reggie lifted his foot from the gas pedal, chewed on his knuckle, and tapped his fingers on the wheel. He reached to turn the dial on the radio, and the car dipped to the left. Then the lights came on.

The stop. The pull. The baton. The crack. The blood. The gurgle. And I don't even know what I was doing, where my body was or why I wasn't covering his, but there was my little brother—body laying on the road, gashes all over. I watched the cop stomp the crown of his scalp, then the back of his head. Reggie screamed and screamed, then stopped altogether. I ran to him. I wanted to be brave but all I could do was howl. I held him and I rocked him.

"Leave it and drive on," the officer said. "Unless you want a turn, too." He spit at the ground beside us, turned, and drove away.

The blood ran everywhere: running all down his face and into his mouth, and then he started throwing it up. I pressed my palms to his head in the places where I could see gashes but it didn't matter, and Reggie didn't notice.

He muttered over and over again, "I can't see anything, Ceiley. Why can't I see?"

Then he was gone. I tried to wake him but couldn't.

When the red and blue lights were far enough away, I pulled him into the passenger side of our sedan and wiped the blood from around his mouth and eyes, they went in every direction. I buried my face into his chest and screamed. I don't remember who called our mother or how we made it to the hospital.

When Mama showed up, saw him unconscious and bloodied, shining in his silver dress, she didn't cry. She didn't say a word to me. She just reached out to hold his hand and shook her head.

A few weeks after the accident, Reggie turned twenty-three and Miss Claudine and Mabel came to visit at the hospital. They brought Reggie chicken salad and long gerber daisies, a pink balloon, and a few magazines. After some time, he was able to sit upright and eat and talk. Most of his front teeth were missing, and the doctors gave him special tinted glasses to keep over his eyes. Mabel set the gifts in front of him and patted his hand with her gloved one. She whispered to my mother, "We'll want the vase back."

"Reggie, I am so so sorry to hear about your troubles," Claudine cooed. Mabel nodded like a puppet.

"We brought you some things to pass the time, some of your favorites to read." Mabel pointed to the stack in front of him. Reggie followed the sound of her heels on the linoleum.

"How thoughtful," I said.

"How are you feeling, dear?" Claudine continued.

"You wanna see what they did to me?" Reggie asked.

Before they could answer, he took his glasses off and his eyes splayed to the side, lazy, his pupils went opposite one another. The room fell silent while we all stared at Reggie. Claudine began to sob.

"Get out," Mama said, standing up. "Get OUT!" She started to shake. I told everyone to leave, and said my brother needed to rest.

When Reggie was in and out on his pain medicine, he'd have this unshakable clarity. He kept asking if the doctor was coming to get him, to take him far away from here, so I started saying, "Soon." Reggie would ask me every morning, "Is he coming today?" and I would always answer, "Soon, Reggie, I promise, *soon*." Nurses told us some sight may return, but it was unlikely. He'd never see anything beyond a shadow in front of his face or sunlight across his eyelids.

One day before he was discharged, he called me over to his bed and gripped my arm harder than he ever had. He took his glasses off and turned his face to me. His eyes floated around.

"I need you to tell me, Celine. Am I still beautiful? Do I look like I can see?"

I held his face. Through his soft grin, I could see the pink of his mouth in between broken teeth. All the little ones were gone now. I brushed some sleep off his face. I looked at Reggie as hard as I could and tried to imagine my brother before, but all I could see was a new him, now.

"Reggie, you are still the most gorgeous thing."

His eyes looped around his sockets. He smiled at me.

"And if I hadn't been there, I wouldn't even know from looking at you that anything was wrong." ❋

THE MIRACLE

Mr. Johnson keeps clearing his throat when Dell Newberry takes the personal call from Ethel on their office line. They're working late, in the middle of a meeting; he's worried about tax season and the return of his largest client, Waco Chicken. Mr. Johnson is gulping Mountain Dew from his Tennessee Guzzler. "Are you sure you called them and followed up?" he asks. Dell nods. He's auditing Dell's records, looking for flaws, but they're spotless. He coughs louder. Dell ignores him, mimes to ask if he's thirsty, then points toward the glass in front of him. This call is important. She's been telling him for weeks she needs time off for the birth. But he'd just looked back at her like she was insane, and said the same thing "It's April, our busiest month. This is your job, Ms. Dell. You're working on my time."

He's dramatic like this. Dell does not care. She's been waiting nine months and seventeen days exactly. She looks at her watch. Her godbaby Barbie should be pushing her own baby, little Lynette, out right *now* and good, here is Barbie's mama, Ethel, on the phone with the news.

"Is she here?" Dell could have jumped from her seat.

Mr. Johnson huffs.

She turns her back to him and smiles into the receiver.

"Ethel? Are you there?"

Ethel sounds very calm on the line when she asks, "Can you do me a favor, Dell? How long would it take you to get to the house from the office?"

Dell's tan Corolla is parked under the pecan tree in the back of the parking lot, and when she gets in, she relocates the hand-ribbon-wrapped gifts for Barbie and baby from the passenger seat to the floorboard behind her. She cranks the engine, turns on the air conditioner, and drives in silence.

Her hands are dry. She picks at a thumbnail and it spreads so far it almost reaches her knuckle. Dell never married, never had children, and lived downtown in a rent-controlled apartment with yellow wallpaper and a yellow couch. She wiped her counters down twice every night, wore her heart on her sleeve, and watched the evening news at 7 p.m. every day. She liked things neat and real particular.

On the phone earlier, Ethel had said Barbie's baby choked to death during delivery. Dell doesn't understand the sentiment at first. *"Ethel what do you mean choked on her way out?"* She can't wrap her head around it. She tries to picture how that worked, but the image in her mind feels too unpleasant.

It'd been twenty-two years since Dell and Ethel were in a women's group together at church, back when Ethel was pregnant with Barbie and her husband ran off. Dell couldn't blame him, honestly. She never liked Ethel much. She was holier than thou, critical, chronically miserable. She didn't expect to know her this long, to be tied to her. But the day Barbie was born, Dell went with the women's group to bring balloons to the hospital, and she got to hold the baby. Barbie was a beautiful baby: wise brown eyes, long fingers. Didn't look anything like her mother. Dell was so smitten and somehow, Ethel saw, and she asked Dell to be the child's godmother. "Of course," Dell said, surprised at how sure she sounded. "Yes, yes."

During Barbie's teen years, Dell mothered her better than Ethel. This was a quiet pride for Dell. When Ethel was insufferable, Dell took Barbie in for a few days to cool off. Barbie's visits turned into sobs, tears soaking in Dell's lap. "Nothing I do is ever enough for her." In moments like this Dell wondered why; why wasn't the girl hers? Why did life turn out this way?

"She loves you, I promise," Dell would tell Barbie.

"She can't say it, but she does. She can't show it. Some people hide their hearts."

"Who am I to question the Lord?" Ethel repeated like a record on the phone, her voice high and thin like a feather. When Ethel pushed, the placenta came out first and ripped, causing the baby to breathe in all the blood tissue on her first breath. "They don't know. They said they can't always explain it. And after the delivery, Barbie went into a catatonic state," Ethel said. Dell replayed the scene that Ethel had described: No reaction, no crying or screaming or asking to hold little Lynette, just big moon eyes that locked on the ceiling. "She can't speak at all, Dell," Ethel explained coolly. "I called her name a dozen times and she couldn't hear me, she didn't even look over at me. It's like she went mute and cracked in two."

In the car, Dell tried not to think about Barbie. *But what about the damn Daddy?* Dell thinks. The baby's good-for-nothing father, Roger Lovelady, hasn't even left work at Sam Turner's tire shop on the other side of town, where he's pulling a double. Ethel said she called and called but the line just kept ringing.

Last year, before Barbie knew she was pregnant and before Roger moved in, Dell got the courage to finally warn her. Dell listened to the girl's lovers' quarrels without judgment, but lately she'd been having nightmares of Barbie calling for her help alone somewhere in the dark. When they met for one of their weekly lunches, Dell was unusually blunt. "I've had it, and I can't hear any more. I think you should leave Roger. He's rotten to his core." It was one of the few things Dell and Ethel agreed on.

Roger lived with his mama in Mechanicsville and worked on cars, mostly. He looked almost translucent, so fair he shimmered like milk-light. He was stout and had fat fingers, his left pointer gone from a welding accident. With flat, black eyes that couldn't hold contact, he talked with a nervous quickness. "There's something funny about him, Dell. He don't settle right with me." Ethel whined over the phone often. "He's nasty too. Quiet as it's kept, I heard he likes spitting in women's mouths."

Barbie was used to excusing abuse. Her mother hadn't ever hit her but she'd never said a kind word to her either. And while Roger had his rough parts, his soul was good, she swore. Barbie wouldn't give up on him; and when they were alone, she saw the real Roger. He was funny, could sing and paint. He never forgot her birthday, always bought her fresh flowers and tiny trinkets, leaving her to wonder where this devil side of his came from. Roger, when he wasn't physical, was at least sweet.

Last summer he kicked her down the stairs and broke her jaw. When Dell tried to get Barbie to leave him, Barbie cried that Dell was overreacting. She'd slipped, she said, and fell on the back porch stairs while coming in from her raised beds.

"I'm telling you, the hose made the steps slick, I didn't even notice."

"You must think I'm stupid, dont you?" Dell asked.

"Be easy on him." Barbie's jaw had looked as blue as lapis.

Dell knew people thought Roger could not be held accountable for his actions because his mind was not fully there. Some people called him special.

And Roger was special. Dell had heard the stories most of her life. Roger died and came back to life when he was nine years old after he drowned.

It was August, 1976, and his parents took him and his brothers to the Holston Hills pool to cool off, but some people started complaining of "coloreds" dirtying their water. Roger's daddy got into a fist fight with some of the men near the snack shack. People ran to break them up. Roger was not a strong swimmer, and as he chased after a yellow rubber submarine toy that kept jetting out his reach, his arm slipped out of his floaty.

His older brother found him face down near the 12-foot marker, still as a baby doll.

They pulled him out. But he had no pulse and was not breathing. After three minutes of no heartbeat, the medics pronounced his passing, his time of death at 2:27 p.m. But his daddy wasn't having it. He screamed at Roger to come out of death and kept breathing into his tiny mouth and pressing on his chest. Roger's mother tried to get him to let it alone—she was afraid he'd crack the child's sternum—but he refused.

He kept pushing and pushing and eventually Roger blinked his eyes and threw up pool water on the concrete floor.

He sobbed. He asked for his Momma. He said he had seen angels.

The whole place fell silent. The housewives whispered all summer long about his resurrection.

There was no denying the miracle. But it came with a consequence. Roger Loveday walked around half-dead from then on.

In the car, Dell looks at the clock. Roger gets off in an hour. He's hoping for a son.

As soon as Barbie found out she was pregnant, he turned into honey. He started rubbing her feet, asked about her day, and brought her tea in the morning before he went off for work.

"You're so beautiful with my baby," he told her. "He really wants this baby," Barbie kept telling her mother and Dell.

Dell has careful instructions from Ethel on where to put things. She pictures what she must do: grab the key under the wicker rocker on the porch, rush up those damn stairs, and rip everything off the walls. She's to load the quilts, baby clothes, and doily baby book into the trunk of her car, throw away the bottles and pacifiers, and push the padded crib into the attic. Dell doesn't quite understand why Ethel wants her to do all this. She knows how sentimental Barbie is, how she's saved every birthday card since she was seven; she'd want to see what had awaited her baby girl. It would make her feel better. "I can come straight to the hospital, tell her I'll be right there," Dell said, grabbing her keys, but Barbie pushed back. "What I need you to do is what I already said. Please get to the house as soon as possible, I've got it handled with my daughter." Dell wanted to slap her through the line. *How cruel could she be?* But she listened. She did what Ethel said. She always did what Ethel said.

It'll take her an hour, at least. How much time did she have? It's a quarter to six. Traffic runs bumper to bumper. The house is fifteen miles away and in this traffic, it might take another hour. And there's no other option. Barbie's new condition isn't covered by insurance. She's coming home tonight; no way could she afford to stay over.

Dell swears at her quivering hands and bangs on the steering wheel. She looks down at her bouncing knees and realizes she tore a rip in her new control nylons.

Dell keeps thinking what Ethel said: "Barbie will have to learn to trust Him in all things."

Dell had hoped to hear a crack in her voice, some sense of sorrow, some gentleness but she didn't. "This is a test of long suffering she must endure." Who would comfort Barbie?

As she weaves through traffic, Dell asks for forgiveness silently. Her flashers are on but people aren't getting out of the way. She doesn't get very far. She didn't tell Mr. Johnson where she was going, only that there was an emergency. She considers pulling over, finding a phone booth, calling him since he only stared at her in silence as she grabbed her bag and left his office while Ethel was on the phone, dryly walking her through what happened. Even though she'd rather turn the other way, go to the hospital and hold Barbie, she will keep her promise to

Ethel. And she will be there for Barbie because no one else can be there like she can.

Dell does not want to think about where Lynette is now. So she thinks about Lynette's name—how Barbie picked it because it meant the place above where God dwells, because she already worshiped her. She thought about the letters she'd sewn into a pale pink sweater.

Dell Newberry's first name is Day. Day Dell Newberry. She was born at dawn—right when the sun was breaking, she was placed in her mother's arms for the first time. Her mother said it felt like God was tending to her heart personally. Dell's mother struggled with big waves of sadness most of her life, which was not expected from such an even-keeled woman. She had these episodes that left her with cuts on her arm from safety razors and burn marks up and down her thighs from her hot comb. But when she was pregnant with Dell, her spirits lifted. Something changed. She grew brighter, telling everyone God brought her light back.

Too bad for Dell that she was a needy and nervous child, and while the sound of a baby crying had not done so, the sound of Dell crying as a "big girl" triggered something deep inside her mother, a reminder of how much she wanted her own caretaking. The darkness returned. This, of course, made her resent Dell and hold her as little as possible. Around the age of three, she started calling Dell by her middle name—no more Day.

Once during one of her blackouts, she'd pinned Dell down and burned her thigh with an iron. The doctor gave Dell's mother lithium, which helped with the self-inflicted harm, but it made her tearful, resulting in hours long bouts of crying in her wingback, salmon-colored chair. Dell hated that color.

Dell takes the Spring Street exit just as the sun goes down. The neighborhood street lights that still worked are clicking on. Barbie and Roger had moved to this side of town after they were married.

Dell swerves through traffic and rolls the windows down. She's so sick she worries she might vomit in her seat.

Ethel was not pleased Barbie would have a baby out of wedlock, but thought the baby could bring some maturity to her hopeless child. Ethel insisted they get married.

It was Dell who helped Barbie get ready for the wedding. "Don't mind her. This is about you," Dell said to Barbie as they shopped for Roger's outfit at Proffitt's. Barbie wanted Roger in a baby blue suit with a navy tie.

"I just wish she could be excited for me and the baby," Barbie said. Dell held Barbie's hand.

The men's clothing was laid out neatly, with cotton shirts pressed and folded in plastic to hold their shape. Ties with mountains, brooks, bass, carp, or cranes were in style, along with wide, French dress shirts. Barbie was excited about the wedding. Dell put in a special request for her pastor Reverend Charlie to marry Barbie and Roger outside of the altar. They would get married in the Smoky Mountains right outside the primitive Baptist church, and afterward, Roger would be born again in the cold mountain water.

At a red light, Dell has to slam on her brakes. The gifts roll under her seat—a pink-and-cream-striped baby bonnet grazes Dell's ankle.

Marriage was never in the cards for Dell. She was not fond of men, did not want to be told what to do, and had no desire for them. She loved one person once. A man she met when she was thirteen and he was twenty, with his long hair straight as a board and slick as silk. He worked at Tam's Drugs, where she would go to buy her mother Tab and pick up her prescription. When he started not charging her for the pop, he wanted to talk to her for a long time, which gave Dell the courage to pass him a note across the cash wrap. In it, she'd drawn him a spicebush swallowtail. They had sex three times in his orange Pinto. At first, she liked how he touched her, then she didn't. The next month, when it was time, Dell didn't bleed in her panties. When she started having to hide her belly, she stopped going to see him at the gas station.

Her mother picked her up from school one day and the two of them drove in silence to Atlanta for the procedure in someone's house. The memory of that isn't so clear. The abortion left her with so much scar tissue, nothing could hold on inside her: She couldn't even stick in a Tampax.

She remembered something, though, the one thing her mother said on the whole ride home: "This is what happens to fast girls."

When Dell turned thirty, she made a bargain with God to get it out of her system and try one last time. She took a trip on her own to San Francisco and paid $60 under red neon lights for a man to take her to a room and make her feel good. All she asked him to do was hold her. No one's touched her since.

When Dell finally pulls her car up to the house, parks, and puts the emergency brake on, she sees blue and pink balloons tied to the handle of the front door. A sign reads WELCOME BABY!

Dell has to make this right.

She races up the front door and starts popping all the balloons. She feels like a lunatic. She doesn't care. She jabs them with her pocket knife, the popping noise throbs in her eardrums. Neighbors hear, come on their porches and watch her, but they don't offer any help. She looks all over for the key to the front door. It's not under the wicker rocker, like Ethel said. She crawls to the door mat, no luck, throws it to the side in the gardenia bushes. She asks the Lord to help her get it done in time.

On her hands and knees, she scrambles. The mailman putters by and a dog barks next door.

Dell thinks she hears a car pull up, an engine cut, and a door slam. Work boots on the pavement, maybe. Her whole life, that feeling. Something bad is coming. Day Dell Newberry glances over her shoulder, but no one is there.

While kneeling, she sees Barbie in her mind's eye just the day before. They checked her delivery bag, talked about her hopes and dreams. Dell listened to the baby kick. How happy Barbie looked, those same wise eyes bright and hopeful.

"Roger finally loves me, Dell," Barbie said, putting her hands on her stomach. Dell tried to smile, but she felt a strange tightness around her mouth. "He said he will be better now. He promised. Everything's gonna be really different now." ✳

KEEPING NOISETTES

Lucille stood in her kitchen and wondered when it would ever stop. She looked out onto the street and watched the rain fall over the telephone wire and flicker through the street lamp glow. It rained sideways, drenching the earth with the oncoming of a fertile spring, for which she was grateful. Lucille wanted full, plush rose bushes this year. In the catalog description, the Noisettes looked impossibly lush.

If she was honest, Lucille desired as vibrant of a pink as possible, the brightest on the block. She put her kettle on the stove top and fidgeted with a tea bag while she re-adjusted her feet on the floor mat. From the kitchen sink she could see a clear shot into Darla Boatright's place, where every possible light was turned on. Inside, Darla chatted loudly with her husband and sipped on a glass of red wine in a crystal flute. She thumbed the remote and changed the TV channels standing up, her back against a white door frame. Darla floated back and forth in a yellow silk robe and matching turban. When she sat in her husband's lap and began licking his neck, Lucille peeled away.

She took in the sensation around her, then turned and looked at her possessions: the faded plaid couch, the floral wallpaper, the modest wooden and glass coffee table from the swap meet. She looked back out the window and felt the warmth of the cup in her hand waning. She looked closer: the rim of the mug had a small chip.

Thirty years ago, when Lucille was eleven, her own father would have pulled her and her sister from their bed to wake and listen, to appreciate the pure delight of hard rain on a tin roof. "It's not much but it's enough. It only takes a little to be satisfied," her father said. Her daughter, Mary, used to stay up with her and watch the rain on nights like this, but now there was distance. She went down the hall and fell asleep without so much as a goodnight.

Lucille gave her space. At sixteen Mary was no longer effervescent. Now she was brooding, beginning to catch on to all that was awful in the world. At Mary's last check-up, a nurse had given Lucille a pamphlet about this behavior, a warning of what was to come. There were pictures of menstrual pads, beer bottles, and condoms.

The title read: *Preparing For Hormones: How to Preserve Your Daughter's Integrity.*

There was nothing Lucille hated more than a loose woman. Even worse was a grown loose woman who was old enough to know better. It signaled lack of restraint, a lack of morality. She looked out the window at Darla Boatright. Those who didn't hold themselves higher, who lacked a strong sense of self-awareness—what a pity.

Darla Boatright was one of those women who rode her husband with the blinds only half drawn, then walked around the cul-de-sac, as if to say, "Oh you didn't see that, did you?" At Darla's thirty-fifth birthday picnic last year she'd worn slacks so sheer, Lucille could make out the pink polka dots of her underwear. She watched Darla's patterned behind all evening while Darla set out trays of ribs, corn on the cob, and ambrosia.

Lucille was mostly happy. And Lucille was trying to be grateful. Years of bitterness settled in a deep crease between her eyebrows. She always looked disappointed.

But she loved her job at the library, and lately she was reading *Invisible Man* before bed. There was a feeling things were going well enough. But she couldn't keep Mary's interest anymore. Lately she'd been keeping her own company in her bedroom with her door closed. Lucille couldn't really get on her too bad, as she was doing exactly what she was supposed to do—getting good grades, volunteering, being on time for curfew— but Lucille could tell she was learning about things that would change her, and she wished she could warn her.

How could she protect her? Each day she imagined Mary's innocence draining further.

Janet told herself she'd knock on one door that night and the right person would open it.

For half the year, she'd bounced from town to town, trying to put down roots. She'd had some luck and been to a string of nowheres and knowns: Columbus, Kannapolis, San-Antonio, Nashville, West Palm Beach. During her travels she'd kept a journal, in hopes of romanticizing her quarter-life crisis. She imagined reading to large crowds about her times all across America. The logs consisted of what she saw, who she touched, where she went, what she ate.

Before Lucille's, Janet negotiated a long stay in a velvet-draped carriage house with ironed linens. Every night a lonely quarter moon shimmered on the walls in her home through the window. She'd met a lawyer at a train station in Charlottesville who offered her a week of no-strings-attached leisure at his estate. *Beauty is a power,* she wrote in all caps in the margins of her journal.

Her own mother warned her many times about altruistic gifts. *There's no such thing as a free lunch.* So, three months ago, when Janet watched the Charlotteville lawyer-husband make his way across the lawn to the carriage house and knock on her bedroom in the early morning, she quickly oiled her legs and took him in stride.

In every town she went to, pretty was her expertise and

curse. Families opened their homes and fed and clothed her well, children clung to her, husbands held too tightly, and kind wives gently corrected her, then gave her the boot. She was a wanderer but didn't have to be. She had a family that loved her somewhere.

Janet chose Lucille's door because of her sad-looking rose bushes. They made her feel better about herself. Her grandmother kept the same ones for years when she was coming up.

Knocking lightly, Janet squared her shoulders and pulled her back straight. The rain fell through her wig and caused her clothes to stick to her like a second skin. Her make-up was sideways and melted down her oval face.

Lucille came to the door with a blank stare. She opened the front door but kept the screen shut and latched between her and Janet. Lucille stared while a bolt of lightning ran across the sky. The young lady looked awfully sad. Lucille pulled her cardigan closer and pinched it shut. She'd taken off her bra earlier in the evening, her nipples hardened from the cold. She felt them like marbles on her palms. Heat rose in her cheeks.

"Sorry to knock so late, could you let me in?"

Lucille scanned her up and down and said nothing.

"May I use your phone?"

"Excuse me?"

"I got off at the bus stop down the street and realized I had the wrong one. It was too late to get back on." She held her hand out, but when Lucille did not offer hers, Janet's fingers grazed the screen.

"I'm Janet."

"Okay. Do you live in town?"

"I do. I live further east." She looked down.

Janet wiped rain off her face forcefully, making the water slap on the front step.

"Can I please just come in and dry off? I can't find a pay phone. The last bus has run. I'm not sure where else to go."

Janet wore a white wool dress with a mandarin collar and sheer stockings. Her body was plump as if she ate well. Her cheeks were rosy with a glow and she held her leather pocketbook in her hands. Lucille thought of Mary standing on a stranger's step and let the girl in, asked her to take her shoes off, and led her to the washroom, where she laid out some of her old pajamas. While Janet put on warm clothes, Lucille spoke through the door.

"I don't usually do this. You can sit with me and have some tea when you're done if you like. And you're welcome to stay the night. It's late now. You can leave in the morning. My name is Lucille, and I live here with my daughter Mary."

"Thank you, you won't even know I'm here."

Janet planned to ask for towels and a washcloth like she usually did, but a set was already there, neatly folded on the back of the toilet. *They must have company often,* she thought. She stripped her clothes off and looked at her swollen belly. She'd felt bloated for days. Climbing into the shower, she took the washcloth and lathered it with soap. She took her wig off, let her hair down, and wiped the dirt off her body, wringing the last week down the drain. She looked over her toes and noticed her stomach looked larger than the day before. She turned around and looked up at the vent fan, the water ran down her back.

In her living room, Lucille paced, pinching the skin beneath her wrist. Why did she let her into her house? Another one? Darla Boatright's lights were off.

It was close to midnight. Mary needed to be up by 6 a.m. for school, and Lucille would have to be at work before the doors opened at 8:30. She poured herself another cup and sat on the couch, listening to hear the water cut.

Mary awoke the next morning to a new one in her living room: Janet asleep in a still line, her hands crossed in an X on her chest. Mary skipped her oatmeal, went into her mother's bedroom and silently threw her hands up.

"I know. I know," Lucille whispered while she lotioned her left leg. She lay back on the bed and sucked in with force, then wrestled her slacks up her thick thighs. "She was out there in the rain, and I'm just helping her. She's leaving this afternoon."

"Mom, you're not everyone's savior. This is getting ridiculous. Do you want these people to murder us in our sleep? It's a matter of time."

"I know I'm not everyone's savior," Lucille said to an empty room.

Mary huffed in the kitchen now, making breakfast loudly, the pots and pans banged, the cabinet slammed.

From the hall, Lucille heard Janet's voice too, the two of them now talking, Mary asked Janet questions. Janet asked Mary questions. Lucille heard Mary let out a stifled laugh. She peeked around the corner, and watched them sit at the kitchen table and eat with their heads down.

Mary sat diagonal from Janet with folded arms while they buttered limp pieces of Wonder Bread. Janet's hair was tied down in a satin scarf, and Mary watched while she ate slowly. Janet wore one of her mother's old T-shirts from Spelman. Janet tried to make conversation with Mary, but she'd only muttered back one-word responses to her questions.

Back in her room, Mary locked the door behind her and flopped on the bed, then watched the ceiling fan. Lucille walked around, back and forth, and Mary watched her feet move back and forth on their hard-wood floors. In the evenings when her mother couldn't sleep, Mary would see Lucille's feet outside her door. She knew what her mother was doing—knew her mother had her hands cupped to her ear on the door, listening in. Mary imagined torturing her mother with deep-throated moans, but she didn't.

Because there were too many hurdles to jump though, Mary had no friends. Her mom was a ruthless judge of character; no one ever seemed good enough. Mary went to school, did her work, and spent her time in her room, reading or practicing laying still, pretending she was in a long rosewood casket. She'd stopped talking and started nodding along with everything her mother said. *Mhmm. Mhmm. Mhmm.* Sometimes she nodded to herself in the mirror for practice. Lucille saw agreement as Mary's admission of respect, that she was always right. In Mary's mind, she saw her mother as the loneliest woman in the world.

Underneath her bed, she'd stuffed admissions letters that had been coming in. Lucille gave her an option of where to go—state schools only—but she had big ambitions beyond the Carolinas. It seemed like she'd never get away from home, though. Her one moment to fade, to not be under so much scrutiny, was when her mother took on her projects. Only then did she become a ghost girl haunting the house, free to vanish. With Janet, Mary indulged some and wondered if this would be different. At worst, she'd disappear for a few weeks. At best, maybe, she could find a friend.

It started with Evangeline, a tall, strange, large-headed young woman who came into the library to cool off during a heat wave and wound up sleeping on their sofa for a few weeks. On a Tuesday, Evangeline stole Lucille's heirloom jewelry and jade china.

Then there was Baby Sara with sienna ringlets who was running from her father. When Lucille bathed the girl she saw cigarette burns down her back. For days, Lucille hid her in the house, making her cinnamon sugar bread for breakfast and bringing home whatever candy she wanted after her work shifts. Lucille held her at night while she whimpered in her sleep. One night while Lucille and Mary slept, Sara left—no note, no anything. She didn't even shut the back door all the way behind her.

In her most recent generosity, Lucille took in an elderly neighbor, Geraldine, who couldn't afford her mortgage. Her retirement money ran out and her children wanted to sell her home, cash in on its equity, and put Geraldine in a state home for the indigent. Instead, she stayed and lived out her last days, enjoying sun on the back patio sipping ice water. One day she died right there in the glider, her neck hung to one side and her eyes open, baking in the heat. Lucille found her after rigor mortis set in, ghastly white and still. Paramedics came and got Geraldine before Mary made it home from school. Lucille was planning the memorial service, fussing over logistics and flyers, when Mary came into her room and sat at the end of the bed. She reached and held her mother's hand.

"Mama, you barely knew her. You don't have to do all that. You don't have to do all that to know you're good."

Lucille figured with some molding she could make something of Janet, but her roses were not blooming like she hoped they would. She checked on them daily, adding a dab of fertilizer, deadheading, but their foliage was dull. Their color lackluster, a gray-flesh pink. Darla's roses were better, bolder, bigger. From her front garden bed, Lucille glared at them. In her housecoat and rollers she picked off dead parts of her blooms, asking them to grow back stronger.

Janet spent her days getting smarter, watching Lucille toil in her garden. Lucille kept telling Janet she had a lot of potential, which Janet wanted to take as a compliment. But Mary looked at her mom with a sour look when she said it. Janet had a bad feeling about it—took this as Lucille crowing at her, implying she was dumb. "She talks out both sides of her mouth," Mary whispered one night in the living room. That's how it went with Lucille and her double-edged parables. Her words always had one million meanings. Sometimes Janet would pronounce something wrong and Lucille would giggle, "Oh, Janet, you're so cute," then correct her.

There were three state schools in the area and Lucille could get Janet enrolled at the community college after she passed her GED. Mary was starting dual enrollment classes and was excited for Janet to come and learn with her. But what would Janet look like in class at thirty-one years old? She didn't finish high school, but that never seemed to be an issue until now. It hadn't occurred to Janet to be something to be ashamed about.

"You can't earn pretty. It's worthwhile to earn something. That's what makes one's life meaningful, a life of the mind," Lucille said in one of her lectures at the dinner table. Janet worked her way through stacks of books Lucille brought home. So far she'd made it through two of the seven, *Sense and Sensibility* and *The Awakening*. She saw herself in both, but most admired Edna Pontellier. "But whatever came, she had resolved never again to belong to another than herself." When Janet slowed down, she realized how much she hated depending on others, but it was the only strategy she knew. She wanted to keep her options open, be free to come and go as she pleased.

Fourteen days passed with more rain. Janet wrote in her journal. *"Somehow I'm still here and it seems like she wants me to be."*

It had been a month since Janet arrived at Lucille's. Each day began to feel like a drag. She'd been waking up through the night in deep dread, choking on something invisible that felt wrapped around her throat. To fight the feelings, she'd written passages about springtime in North Carolina, its piercing beauty. Beyond the Noisettes, all around Lucille's yard were vibrant heavens: sunshine-yellow forsythia bushes, bright Persian Silks, syrupy winding ropes of Wysteria, and blinding rows of rhododendrons. With a recent warm front coming in, the women spent the few rain-clear evening hours on the front porch, enjoying the soft breeze. Janet wanted to believe she'd found a small paradise. Somehow Lucille was her long-lost mother, Mary the baby sister she'd never had. But she had all those things somewhere else, and their love didn't require her changing much.

Every other week Lucille worked on Saturdays for overtime. On the third Saturday she'd been there, Janet wandered through the neighborhood, peeking through everyone's bay windows. As families sat down for dinner, she felt an ache inside. On her third lap around, Darla Boatright appeared on her front porch in a peach duster, waving.

"Hey, darling!" Janet knew she should keep walking, she'd heard so much about "nasty Darla," but she ignored Lucille's better judgment and walked over anyway. Darla's house was large and cool with dark wood paneling and a fireplace. Her husband was out, she said. She asked Janet to walk with her over to the kitchen, where she grabbed some puppy chow and poured them glasses of sherry. Janet noted the soft glitter powder across Darla's décolletage, her black irises rimmed with soft blue rings, how warm yet uncomfortable Darla made her feel. Her eyes were circled with an indigo liner that ran in the corners. She kept wiping them like she was crying.

Darla sat next to Janet and stared at her, keeping eye contact much longer than she was used to. They chatted for a while, and Janet did her best to dodge the questions, mostly saying Lucille was an old friend, more like family. Janet noticed how fast Darla talked, how she swished the alcohol around like mouthwash. Janet kept checking her thin gold watch. Lucille would be home soon and she felt ashamed for being at Darla's. Her nerves were on edge as she thought about getting home after her. She felt like she'd done something bad. Janet hoped the visit wouldn't show on her face. After about an hour or so Janet stood up and excused herself, thanking Darla for her hospitality. They hugged.

"You're welcome any time sweetheart. You're just a doll."

"Thank you, Darla. You've got a lovely home. I better get back now."

"I mean it, I've got four guest rooms. Anytime."

"I may take you up on that, I appreciate it. Lucille should be home anytime, I need to start dinner."

Janet turned to walk down the stairs, but Darla pulled her closer, squared their bodies together and looked her in the eyes. Janet could smell the sherry on her breath. Darla put her hands on her shoulders.

"Lucille did good with you. She picked well." Darla moved a piece of hair from Janet's cheek behind her ear.

"Excuse me?" Janet's stomach dropped.

"Take it as a compliment, dear. It's refreshing to see one of Lucille's unfortunates actually have some spunk. There's something growing in you that wants to get out. I see a sparkle in your eye."

Lucille liked looking at Janet throughout the day. Through Janet, she remembered the womanhood she had dreamed of when she was younger: the smoothness of her skin, the firmness of her legs, and shine in her hair.

She once was younger and beautiful like that too; silly, unaware, head turning.

Janet was polite and picked up after herself and got on with Mary, but she seemed more to herself lately. They talked about clothes and lipstick, and Janet gave Mary some tips on learning her "season." Mary was a winter; she needed more jewel tones, apparently. While the girls visited, Lucille returned to her rose garden, telling herself to pace herself, not to get too attached to this stranger.

How would she tell people about the new member of her home? She had an estranged half-sister in Michigan, Dorlene, who never visited. She could say this was her niece who was coming to see life in the South. Maybe her sister fell ill. Or she could be the new intern at the library studying under her and assisting with the new curation series she'd be rolling out soon.

A few days later, the rain lifted and the air turned toward summer heat. Lucille's Noisettes dropped further, turning yellow at the corners. A co-worker suggested more worms in the soil; another told her to try coffee grounds to keep pests away. She held a bloom in her palm and touched the edges tenderly with her thumb, then heard some tapping. Darla was knocking on her window and waving to her. Lucille put her hand over her eye, pretending there was a glare. She yanked the hose from the side of the house and turned the water on, flooding the already-wet soil in the hot, morning sun.

Lucille and Janet and Mary settled into a new routine. Lucille would go to work, Mary would go to school, and Janet would stay at home, learning and helping out with the chores. Janet moved off the couch into the spare bedroom. Mary mentioned Janet felt like a sister, which made Lucille happy. They ate supper together and sometimes played cards in the evening. Lucille was feeling so good she brought some rum cake home for the three of them on the weekend, and they all ate the whole thing Friday night. Lucille knew it was quick to say, but inside she felt as if she had two daughters now.

Janet woke up in the middle of the night to run to the bathroom because her stomach was hurting with what felt like cramps but different, more intense. She expected to vomit, as, come to think of it, she'd been nauseous for a few weeks, but she had to sit instead. She wiped and went to flush but the toilet paper felt heavy. She wiped more and more and it still felt wet. She looked back and the toilet was filled with blood. Her period, she guessed. Had she skipped one? She couldn't remember. Would that explain how much blood there was? Surely Lucille or Mary had pads in here. She couldn't find any in the cabinet beneath the sink or the little cupboard below the window. She tried to hold the tissue there as long as she could to soak the bleeding. She looked through her legs and clumps of purple, birth-blue flesh filled the bowl. Goosebumps spread over her arms and legs. Eventually, she padded her underwear with tissues until it fit like a diaper.

The window was small but she thought she could

crawl through it, and for some reason after she washed her hands, she did. She jumped out the window and laid under the bushes, felt the cool grass dew on her back and looked up at the house above her. She closed her eyes for so long she almost fell asleep.

Darla next door knocked loud enough to knock the damn shutters off the house. Lucille looked at the time. It was 4:30 p.m. She was about to put the chicken thighs in the oven, so they could cook in time for everyone's return. Mary would be home around 5:30 from work and Janet was out picking up potato salad for her. She checked on the Pyrex in the oven and walked to the door.

"Darla, what a surprise."

"Oh, Lucille, it smells delish here, I've always admired your down-home cooking."

"What a kind thing for you to say."

Darla adjusted her mauve wrap top and swept her bangs away from her face. Some hair was stuck to her lipstick. She paused.

"How can I help you, Miss Darla?"

"Could I borrow two eggs? I dropped my last two yesterday, I got kinda startled."

"Sure, stay right there and I'll be back."

Lucille closed the screen door between them. She walked to the kitchen and opened the refrigerator, stuck her head in deep and screamed silently, then poked around the eggs.

Darla hollered from the door. "I was startled because I saw your new...tenant, and she spooked me. I saw her poking around your rhododendrons last night! I almost thought she was a burglar if she wasn't so shapely and lovely. Where is she from?"

Lucille gave her two ugly eggs and went to wrap them up.

"Oh, she's my niece, visiting the South for a bit."

"How strange! She looks nothing like you. I didn't know you had a sister."

Lucille handed her the eggs.

"Yeah, I do."

"Well I guess that's none of my business, but I hope she enjoys her visit down here, however long she stays. She seems like a nice girl."

At the grocery store, Janet bought potato salad from the deli counter and then went to the pharmacy where she was planning to buy pads, a heating bottle, and go. But the woman behind the counter looked like she could have been her grandmother, and before Janet could grab anything from the shelves, the woman asked her, "What's bothering you, honey?"

"I'm bleeding. A lot."

"Heavy enough to go through a pad?"

Janet nodded.

The woman walked from behind the counter, shuffling her feet, and Janet saw she had the same SAS black loafers Lucille wore. She walked past the pads and picked up a pregnancy test.

"You need this. And you need to go to the doctor. Today, dear."

At the dinner table, the women sat around passing the sides. Lucille had made a good meal: deviled eggs, potato salad, baked chicken, greens, and butter cake. They ate in silence, except for the clinking of glass and silverware. Janet wore a red bandana on her hair. Lucille thought it looked girlish and stared at it while they ate.

"Girls, guess who brought her behind to the house while y'all were gone?"

"Who?" Mary asked.

"Darla. She needed two eggs for something. Lord knows she didn't."

"That woman is so strange. I have already seen her indecent more times than I asked for," Janet said, shaking her head.

"I know that's right," Mary said, and Lucille smirked, proud.

"But listen to this, Janet. She said she saw you last night out in the bushes or something, looking around. I thought that was so strange of her to say."

Janet poured some more lemonade in her glass. "Oh I couldn't sleep. So I was checking on your roses. Seeing if I could figure out why they looked unwell. With all this rain, you're overwatering them. The roots need to dry out." She took a bite of her greens.

Janet went back to eating her dinner but Lucille put her fork down. She'd never raised her voice with Janet and had only once been direct, firm, when she asked Janet to be mindful of Mary and to please give them notice if she was leaving, but this expression on her face was different.

"Come again?" Lucille asked.

"I wasn't trying to offend you, Ms. Lucille. I was just saying that was the issue. My grandmother kept Noisettes."

Mary hung her head.

"Janet, I'm no fool. Whatever and whoever you chose to spend your evening hours with is none of my concern. But don't come in here lying at my table where I feed you. Those roses are just fine."

On a Tuesday, Janet and Mary played hooky while Lucille worked a double at the library. Mary skipped her summer school lit class. They took the bus downtown to the mall, ate at the food court. Janet kept telling Mary what a great girl she was, how proud she was of her. Mary found it odd.

"I got into college," Mary said.

"Well I know *that*. Your mother's been gloating to everyone about your full ride. Are you gonna live at home or on campus?" Janet asked, poking at her chess pie.

"No, not the state schools. I got into Howard in DC. And I got a scholarship too, tuition and room and board. I just need help getting the deposit together. I can't ask Momma, but my dream is going this fall. I can take the Amtrak straight there."

Janet got real quiet then pulled her wallet out of her purse.

"How much you need?"

The house was tense for weeks after the confrontation over the roses, so Lucille decided to get tickets to see *Fiddler on the Roof*, hoping to smooth things over. They could dress up and get dinner downtown at Grey's. She picked up the tickets from the box office after her shift and hurried home to surprise the girls.

Lucille walked in and put her things away. The house felt large and quiet. Mary was working a new job at the ice cream place up the street for the summer. She would get off work in the next few minutes. She seemed farther away than ever. Just to check, Lucille looked under her bed and found nothing out of the ordinary. It was her house after all. The only new thing was a glass jar filled with cash, the girl's tips.

She walked back to the guest room where Janet slept. She knocked on the door, then after a while, opened it. The bed was made, tucked with hospital corners. Her stack of books sat neatly on the nightstand. The hardwood floors stunk of vinegar. Lucille looked around for Janet's things. She checked under the bed, opened the closet, pulled open every drawer. The window was cracked and the wind was blowing through the white lace curtains. Lucille looked outside, where the summer heat made waves off the pavement. She looked to the front window where her rose bushes were burning in the sun. Lucille was so proud of how full they came in. She'd taken Janet's advice and laid off the hose for a week, and her Noisettes came alive. But now, as June turned to July, their season ended. The remaining few were drooping, bleached out and pale, the edge petals curled in with exhaustion.

Past the roses she saw the sprinkler running in the street, children dancing in the cool water. Darla was on the sidewalk passing out popsicles. Lucille thought she saw Janet, but it was just a neighbor. One girl ran circles around her mama's laundry, her bed sheets waving through the air. She was showing everyone how fast she could go. They all stopped and watched her while she flew, as she opened her arms, as her body bolted like a long black bird under the clotheslines. ❋

HOW TO CUT AND QUARTER

White-tails littered Daddy's yard and grazed in the shadows around the oaks. It looked like a hundred of them. I watched them while I lay on my side, out of breath from my run. It was July and the cicadas were buzzing and I was dripping in sweat. Miss Birdie asked me to meet her at 6 p.m. for dinner—*let's talk things out.* She'd picked us up a movie from the Redbox at Walgreens. She loved the ones with Lauren Bacall or Sophia Loren. She was worried about me, had been calling me for days and I'd kept blowing her off. She left me voicemails: "Hello, Marjorie? This is Birdie. How are you my dear? Don't be like this. Call me please. Wait, is that you? On the other line? I'll get off the line. You might be calling as we speak!" I let the phone ring. She sent me prayer cards, honey candies, and pressed pansies in the mail. She sent me disposable film photos of myself bent over in her garden hat and galoshes tending to the tomatoes. In perfect penmanship on the back, she'd written: *good memories!*

I left them all on Daddy's desk.

A doe leaned down to drink water at the edge of a puddle. It was fresh, so full of little life. Absurd eyelashes, tarry nose. Didn't even notice me watching even though I could fit both my hands around its neck and my fingers would touch. How could anybody crack through those tiny necks then mount them on their wall? I pictured myself separating the tendons from the bone and hoisting up a baby deer head myself. I felt ashamed after. I lay still until the sun set, remembering, feeling the stitch down the length of me start to rip. If I moved at all I'd spill out onto the grass. I'd grease it maroon with my insides. I had a dull ache so big nothing would help it unless something gutted me entirely. I wanted to be carved out with a spoon.

June. I moved home to handle the estate after Daddy passed—car accident or incident, I didn't know what to call it. I was 29, childless, but I had a baby face and zero forehead wrinkles, so some things were working for me. Before I made it down for the funeral I maxed out my Capital One card on dark, high-necked Eileen Fisher linens and thick, round, black bifocals so folks would see me as city-wealthy. I shaved my legs, relaxed my halo, and practiced sitting tall, naked in my bedroom mirror. I looked at my labia and debated which side was longer then I poked my nipples in and watched them pop back out, which made me laugh, until I remembered what I was doing, where I was going.

I packed my bag, making sure to leave anything adorning at home. No blush, no hoop earrings. I took the nail polish off my fingers and toes, left my perfume, and took my necklace off. I was a plain shell of myself. To show up and be welcomed, I couldn't appear to be prideful.

I had no sorrow; I wasn't sure when it would come, if ever.

Daddy pastored a Seventh-day Adventist church right outside of Chattanooga in Collegedale, population 11,000. It wasn't too far from Atlanta where I worked as a junior copywriter, shucking mostly infomercial copy. My daddy joked we were both in the business of persuading people but really, I wondered if he was sad I'd given my life to something without any real meaning.

The day I made it to the house, I stopped into Daddy's study, which was at the back of the house in a sunroom. Things were mostly the same as they would have been. It was airy and bright, with built-ins and a big oak desk. I sat in his chair for over an hour, trying to feel him, before I made my way to the receiving line of friends. His essence lingered, which was the kind of religiously deficient spiritual thing he wouldn't want me thinking. The church taught us that dead was dead until resurrection day. There was his King James leather Bible, a copy of Ellen G. White's *Desire of the Ages*, a small notebook. His water mug was still there, too (he only drank water piping hot, before or after meals), along with his cufflinks and a pack of uneaten peanut butter crackers. There was a broad-racked Rocky Mountain Elk on his wall that Deacon Oscar gave him for his sixtieth birthday. He brought it back for him all the way from Medicine Bow Forest, Wyoming. I stared at it in its glass eyes, waiting for it to offer some consolation.

My mother couldn't make it down for the service. *"I hope you can understand. This is what's best for me."* After the divorce ten years ago, she started seeing a Universal Unitarian therapist, got some courage (read *Codependent No More!*), left the Seventh-day Adventist church, and remarried. Sometimes, after her sessions, she'd slip up and tell me about the other sides of my father: his rendez-vouses, gambling, favorite ladies in the congregation. I didn't believe her. And I couldn't hear it then. *Daddy?* I thought. No way.

Her new spouse, Jax, was stupefyingly kind. They were quiet, made Red Clover tinctures, wore a low ponytail, and barely spoke above a whisper. My mother met Jax at a summer conference for zero-waste living.

They fell for each other quickly and moved to Asheville. With her alimony, they bought a quaint stone cottage on the Swannanoa River. They drank alkaline water, had a tomato garden, got rid of their TV, and read Pema Chödrön before bed. My dad didn't understand. They had something I wanted.

My mom went through a lot after she left my father, after she left the church, so I didn't blame her for not coming. The one thing Mother asked was that I check on Barbara "Birdie" Bowman, her old friend from her days as a pastor's wife. Miss Birdie had to be in her sixties now. When I was little, she was magic, the one thirty-something in our church who was mothering and had still hung on to some youthful vitality. They were so close, Miss Birdie and my mother—always in the kitchen together, going on overnight hikes, running special projects at church—that when I got older I often wondered if there was something more between them. I didn't see any of that as a child. I only saw how keen her senses were, how in tune she was with her children, how they hung from her arms like vines and slept on her lap in church. I wanted the affection that she layered on her children.

When I was a young girl I wanted a mother like Miss Birdie.

Daddy had two through-lines running in him—the public and the private—and the contrast was so jarring that in my mind I had two fathers. In the pulpit he was supernatural, preaching with a hypotonic, staccato cadence that brought the house down. He was tall, bone-thin; he had a wise gaze and strength in his sense of decision, believing a shrewd man said nothing at all.

At home he was reserved, and painfully so. Preoccupied, speaking mostly through body language, we learned to understand him through microscopic changes in his demeanor. The type of man to take pleasure in mental tenacity, he enjoyed fiddling with things rather than talking to his family. We cut him a wide berth. On the weekends he took apart washing machines and put them back together, "stroking his big IQ," my mother would say. Parts of machinery junked up the house. We learned to infer his love from gestures. An offer to pour a cup of coffee was *I love you.* A question about a known recipe was a distant *How are you?* And yet, with all the space around him, he still required more. How he felt about us was up to interpretation—his undying adoration, a figment of my overactive imagination.

While he rose above us in his pearly orbit of solitude, we admired him from earth. For a long time I was convinced if we reached far enough we could touch him, at least skim the hem of his celestial garment, when in reality, he was only always six billion miles away.

The funeral was long and sweltering; I felt trapped in a fever-dream, Tyler Perry trip. Our old-school service was tent-revival style, complete with those old fans with a wooden handle left over from a 2007 Easter service. I saw a fat older lady with a crooked wig sneak a Snickers for her low sugar. She chewed it like a cow on cud and looked around as if she was maintaining her discretion. I started to smile. The pain had me laughing quietly behind my gloved hand and my knockoff Marc Jacobs eyeglasses I bought from a Chinese website. My cheeks kept rising, and I thought my jowls might snap. I'd been to so many funerals Daddy preached over, seen people leap from their seats, dance, fall out at the casket. I thought he'd live forever. My scalp was itching from the relaxer.

I felt my heartbeat around my temples from the tightness of my wide-brimmed death hat.

My Apple Watch buzzed to tell me I was late with a payment. 11 a.m. According to the program, we were just getting through the opening hymns.

There were five pastors from my father's district in Tennessee who were lined up to give a word about his life. Four out of five had on toupées; two out of those four wore seersucker with cream gators and no socks. After their words, there was a solo music break. Aunt Bessie was going to read the condolences then sing "There is Balm in Gilead" (Daddy's favorite) for the offering, followed by the words of friends.

And then, two hours into the service, once everyone was sweating and hungry and needed to pee and without an ounce of attention left, I read my eulogy. I had written a few things but still didn't know what to say. I felt nothing.

I felt nothing through the preachers' words, nothing through the singing, nothing through the moments of reflection. I felt nothing—until one of my daddy's friends told a story about their childhood together, and then I felt my seam come undone. I couldn't catch my breath. I looked from my seat onstage for something to hold on to. Miss Birdie sat on the front row in a matching tweed chartreuse set with a pillbox hat. She looked good for her age—her legs were long and slim and her ankles looked tiny. The white sheen from her nylon stockings looked ashy against her caramel skin. Her legs were crossed. Miss Birdie had on these classic white pumps that were scuffed, and her foot bobbed on rhythm, soothing me like a tide.

When it was my turn, I took every lesson as a preacher's daughter and put it to good use: I had the cadence of a proper eulogy down, the lesser known scripture I'd heard Daddy recite from this very pulpit, with well-timed long pauses and just the right pinch of pathos and just enough restraint. No sobbing for me, not with all eyes on me. I added a few seconds of eye-watering right after the "wild, precious life" Mary Oliver quote, pulled my shoulders back, and ended with something personal and insightful. I beamed as I looked up from the podium, real dignified behind my luxury sunglasses. But everyone looked at me like I was deranged.

I tasted pennies in my mouth. I touched my hand to my nose and saw the white glove fingertips soaked red. It wasn't a dainty trickle. Not one nostril but both pouring blood down my face. There was my feral laughing thing again. A wild, precious laugh? Not a crowd favorite. I got crickets. So I pinched my nose and whispered thank you, stepped down, and re-took my seat. The next time heads were bowed in prayer, I crushed a Xanax between my back molars and gulped down some water then lifted my head back.

Someone sang "In This Very Room," and it could have been the Spirit or the meds, but I swear, finally, I felt the Lord beside me.

Back at Daddy's house, at the potluck, I hid in the bathroom off the guest room and listened with my ear to the door to see if people were talking about me. Sister Hattie yelled at all the ladies to bring the food out. I needed to do something about this swamp ass. I lifted my linen dress and used the blow dryer to fan my pubes off. There was no trash can to throw away my wet panties, so I stuffed them behind the toilet. While on my hands and knees, tucking them out of sight, I saw some splatters of shit on the baseboards and an empty container of preparation H. There were papers, some dusty looking glossy pages in a wicker basket—a magazine with a naked woman and her bare ass cheeks. I picked it up. *American Woman*. That's what it was called. Some of the pages were crusted together. One page that was dog eared opened to a woman spread-eagle with a full bush on a flannel blanket. Patriotic. I didn't want to, but I imagined Daddy sitting on the toilet. I gave Miss American Woman a salute. Someone knocked at the door. Miss Birdie was checking in, cooing me to come out and greet my guests. Everybody was there, waiting for me.

If my mother had been there, she would have said you can only eat so much hash brown casserole. *I can eat as much as I want*. I made it through the meal by never letting the white of my plate show too long. When I ate all the Sister Schubert's rolls, I filled the space with sweet potatoes. Once I ate the greens, I filled the space with chili cheese rice. We Adventists don't eat meat and don't drink. Brother Amos sat in the corner, flapping his legs and looking at me. Sister Deborah watched my plate and smiled at me. I smiled back. She mistook this to be an invitation, walked over and sat beside me, and started rubbing my back. My mother used to do it to me at dinner to help me digest. I hated having my back touched while I ate. She rubbed in circles then up and down. As she talked, my ears went in and out.

"Slow down baby, it's not going nowhere."

Three more waffles.

A piece of Morningstar veggie bacon.

"Your father was such a good man, it's a shame he's gone. He was one of a kind."

White sparkling grape juice.

"But you know, the Lord giveth and the Lord taketh away."

Two scoops of vegan Watergate salad.

"I know you have to miss him. I can't imagine. What

would bring a man his age to take his own life? I know you all told everyone it was a car accident, but something about that don't sit right with me. You know? Going the wrong way on the interstate mid-day?"

Faux turkey.

Parsley garnish.

A whole clove of roasted garlic.

Twenty singular butter mints.

I excused myself from Sister Deborah and complimented her astute gift of ministry and wandered outside to take a walk. At the back of the property, I screamed as loud as I could.

Daddy's land was the one thing about him that made me think he was tender. It was immaculate, full of poplars, black oaks, English ivy, and African violets. You didn't have to be from the country to see that the person who lived here really cared about this place. I paced out there for hours, waiting for all the visitors' cars to clear from the front of the house. I breathed in as much as I could. Last week, in Atlanta after I learned he was dead, it had rained for days. My therapist told me to write stanzas of how this time was shaping me. I wrote in my Notes app some bullshit like, *the world was weeping for me when I couldn't.* "This is not your fault," she told me. "Sometimes people have whole lives, whole worlds we know nothing about."

The end of the property edged on a tiny river. I sat on the bank and watched the water and tried to listen but all I heard was Miss Birdie calling for me.

I stood in the doorway and watched for a minute before she saw me. Miss Birdie was cleaning the kitchen for me. I underestimated her. She had synced her phone up my Bose speaker, and Donnie McClurkin lulled in the background. She had taken off her pumps now and moved through the kitchen in her stockings. Her tweed jacket was draped over a chair at the bar, her wig was off, and her hair was in silver cornrows to the middle of her back. This felt too personal, to see an elder undone like this. I wanted to leave but I didn't. As annoyed as I was to have her there, I was also relieved. She was doing so much for me, and I was grateful. And she made it easy. There wasn't that moment of guessing when a stranger comes over and offers to help with dishes. Nothing in this kitchen had changed since I was a girl. She washed and dried, swept and tidied. She knew where the tricky things went, like the cooking sheets, finer china, the emerald tea kettle. She knew exactly where all the plates and cups went. Exactly. Maybe my mom called her and asked her to stay and look after me, but something felt weird, and I had that knot feeling in my stomach.

Miss Birdie looked fit. I thought she was beautiful in the way a grandmother was. The backs of her arms were sinewy and muscular and suddenly I felt self-conscious. I pinched the back of my arm flab. When everything was clean, Miss Birdie smiled at me and put some nettle tea on the stove. I shook off the funny feeling and texted my mom.

Miss Birdie is great! She's over here now. Very helpful.

I wanted my mom to be there, not this other woman I hadn't spoken to in years. I hoped she got the hint. Exhausted, I laid my head on the granite countertop.

"I'm sorry about Sister Deborah." Miss Birdie placed a cup of tea beside my head on the counter then returned to washing dishes, her back to me.

"Oh, no she was fine, she didn't mean any harm."

"Lord help her rubbernecking."

I smiled, put my chin on my hands and looked up at her. She smiled over her shoulder, an eyebrow lifted as if to say: *Come on.*

"Okay sure, I was getting pretty annoyed. And is it just me or does her breath smell... interesting?"

"Oh, baby, you mean that roadkill ammonia smell?"

I coughed at her sharpness, smiled even wider.

"Like a rat had crawled up there and died. It's a shame."

Miss Birdie walked over and poured herself a glass of nettle tea, too, then stared at me kinda funny. From the freckles under her eyes, to the fullness of her upper lip, Miss Birdie sure had the loveliest features.

After Miss Birdie left to walk home, I spent the whole night out of my body, thinking of that *American Woman* magazine I found. I considered my father's other lives. Maybe he was a fisherman, a Chippendale, a painter.

Maybe he didn't want to be known by me. I lay in the guest room running over the day. I watched *Next* on MTV2, eating speared dill pickles two at a time. Vinegar dripped into my breasts. I checked the clock, looking for Angel Numbers, a sign that Daddy was at peace or made it safely to the other side. I wanted to see 2:22 (new beginnings) or 5:55 (gray clouds in your life are about to be sent away). I would have settled for 11:11 (It's time to manifest the life you want!). It was 2:39 in the morning.

The next day Miss Birdie came by and met me on the porch with a citronella candle and a bottle of Red Passion Alizé. I didn't think she drank, but here she was, pouring us two heaping mug fulls.

"How you holding up?" She said it like a whisper. Her dimples could hold pennies.

"Fine. I guess. Just trying to make it through."

"I know, baby. It's hard." Her eyes locked with mine. "You know, I'm sure it must be so lonely in that big house you're staying in. I was thinking. See my son Edward is in town, he's studying for his LSAT, working as a tutor at UT Chattanooga for the summer and he can watch the house. Knowing his manish behind, he'd probably want the privacy."

I nodded. I remembered Edward from high school. We barely spoke. He'd been one of the few students in the country who scored a perfect 36 on his ACT. Birdie and her husband Charles were all over the newspaper when he got into Dartmouth. Charles, an oil and gas tycoon, was sixty-five when he married Birdie at twenty-five. He passed the summer before my freshman year of college. I heard from my mother, who heard from my father in passing that none of Birdie's family came to the funeral.

"And I hate knowing you're in that big house all by yourself. It just don't sit well with me. I wouldn't be a good mama if I left you there alone. So why don't I come and stay with you for a bit? At least the first week. I can make the meals and help clean up. You won't even know I'm there."

My Daddy was from Mechanicsville, and so was his daddy, who, orphaned and alone, somehow made a way for himself. First as a pilot in the Korean war, then by farming dairy cattle and soybeans. He had a small drinking problem. Who wouldn't? He liked his house quiet. Any noise after he'd been drinking would make him rage. Daddy's whole family—sisters, aunts and uncles were quiet like he was. Once, I asked my mother how they met, and other than the church having something to do with it, she couldn't really remember much, only recalled the date she went to meet his parents. They ate at Great American Steak & Buffet then went back to the house for dessert. "Everyone sat on the porch in complete silence. It was deafening. They just rocked, smiled and rocked," she told me. "I was stumped. I tried to ask questions and they just kept rocking and nodding. I kept looking at him to see if this was normal, and he wouldn't really look back at me. Hours went on like that. Our wedding was so quiet it felt like a wake."

As a little girl I tried my hardest to *get* Daddy. The more I talked, the bigger our chasm became. Every word he gave me felt like a private treasure like a morsel of cake, or water after a fast. Once, after a late revival, me and daddy drove back to the parsonage in his station wagon. I pretended to sleep, closing my eyes and feeling the wind on my face from the window, hoping to make myself limp enough to be carried when we got inside. Then Saddy started singing "There is a Quiet Place:" "There is a quiet place / Far from the rapid pace / where God can soothe my troubled mind / Sheltered by tree and flow'r / There in my quiet hour with Him / my cares are left behind."

So pure and pretty like a bird, like a roaring river let loose from a dam. For the forty-five-minute ride through the plateau, I imagined my eyelids threaded shut. I pinched my eyes so hard, strawberry stars burst in my vision. We hit a bump in the road that caused me to shoot up, gasping for air. He stopped singing immediately, and as I tried to go back to sleep, I prayed for one more note. He didn't open his mouth for the rest of the ride.

Her first night after she moved in, Miss Birdie cooked a stir fry for dinner and sat next to me on the sectional. We watched the Oprah Winfrey Network and crunched on our snap peas covered in sesame oil. I could hear her molars smacking down, gently, as she chewed. She'd taken her shoes off, curled up close to me.

A family on the screen was navigating a dark secret. *"Demarcus, a music producer, wants to come clean to his wife about his second family. Demarcus has three other children by two women. He needs to stand in his truth and speak to his wife about his real intentions."*

During a commercial break, Miss Birdie popped Jiffy corn and rolled a quarter stick of butter through. She put it in a green bowl that had my thumb prints in red paint pressed around the rim. It was a Christmas gift for Daddy I worked hard on in my third grade art class. He had been away in Oregon studying for his doctorate in divinity. He went three times a year for his residency and stayed with Uncle Oscar, a Danish Adventist pastor visiting on an education visa who kept a starkly clean house with only gray, white, or cream decor. Small, European-looking trinkets like pom-poms or angry-looking reindeer figurines lined the walls. I knew what it looked like from the Polaroids Daddy brought back. When Daddy came home for Christmas that year, I gave him the bowl; I had wrapped it myself. That year I took a photo for the Christmas parade at school. I wore my hair in braids with bobbles at the end. When I went to put my picture in his wallet as a surprise, to replace the old one, I saw the same old things: a picture of him and my mother on their honeymoon in Portugal, a Polaroid of him and Uncle Oscar and his Divinity cohort on the lake, the two of them holding a big bass. But in what had always been my spot toward the back of the billfold, I was gone, replaced by a picture of a blonde woman in a white button-down laying on a dock at Lake Michigan, the sun shining in her wide, green eyes. I must have known, even as a child, what it meant. But I shut the wallet, willing myself to forget, taking my own picture back to my bedroom.

As the days grew the hotter I rose early, with the sun.

Every woodland creature, it seemed, found their solace in Daddy's backyard. Wisteria crawled up the gates now, so fragrant, and I heard bullfrogs in the evening singing, attuned with the woodpeckers' cadence.

Miss Birdie threw us a solstice party; she made violet lemonade and Black Forest cake to celebrate the longest day of the year and pretend it didn't mean we were soon returning to darkness. As we spread out on a quilt in the grass, I pressed into the glass I was sipping off and took a deep breath. Miss Birdie laid on her stomach, crossing her delicate feet together at the ankle, a tiny gold anklet draping there. I saw the twinkles of tattoos, a half moon with a face, a fairy wand, a few splashes of magic glitter. She had her silver hair piled up on top of her head with a tortoise-shell banana clip. I didn't feel the knot anymore when we were together. As we sipped the lemonade, the violets we picked turned the sweetest pink as they settled in with the acidity. She moved some hair out of her face. I pulled my sun hat down over my eyes.

In Atlanta, after work on Fridays, I went to Los Amigos with my co-workers Matt and Jen for their jumbo margarita special. The last time I saw them was the day I got the call from my mother, who got the call from Miss Birdie, that my father had been in an accident on the interstate. He was going the wrong direction. His Cadillac hit the barrier wall in the median and ricocheted into a culvert. Later, anyone I talked to—my mother, the EMT, my therapist, my roommate—seemed compelled to tell me this type of impact was "*quick and painless.*" I took the call an hour before we were going to leave for the restaurant while I was in the second-floor bathroom of the office, trying to dump out my menstrual cup. I put myself on mute, released umber clots down the toilet. "He's dead, baby. I'm so sorry. He's dead." I hung up the phone, felt flat, my ears muffled like I was underwater. I went back to my desk. I ordered a new dress on Amazon, googled bullet bras, chatted with cubicle mates, made a list of what I wanted to get at Food Lion.

At Los Amigos, Jen and Matt and I were playing two truths and a lie, and all I could see was the Cadillac flipping in my head. My phone kept buzzing. Matt downed two twenty-four-ounce Dos Equis and revealed he went to furry conventions. Jen admitted she tried crack once and—she said it was related but I wasn't sure how—that she didn't like what she looked like with her clothes off. We ordered a round of jumbo peach margaritas, and then it was my turn. "I'm six foot four. I'm from Denmark.

My father was in a car accident earlier today. He's dead. He was going the wrong way on the interstate," I said, waiting for them to guess. They didn't say anything. So I leaned in closer, shaking like a dog, lifting off the booth seat and hovering in toward their faces. My hair dripped into the cheese dip.

"HE WAS GOING THE WRONG WAY ON THE INTERSTATE, CAN YOU BELIEVE IT?" I think I was yelling because everyone in the restaurant looked over at our table. The manager started walking our way. Matt offered to take care of the bill. Jen said she'd drive me home.

"Okay." I said. "Okay, that's okay."

I had been putting off cleaning out the house for weeks. The parsonage deferred to my mother, but she signed off on the paperwork and deferred it to me. Either I would keep it and put my name on the deed or I could turn the home back over to the church. I wasn't sure if I wanted to go back to Atlanta. I took a leave of absence from work. I was here, for now. I couldn't make that decision yet, so I stress-cleaned. In the study, I moved with a heaviness in my legs. Starting with file cabinets, I pulled out bins and thumbed through manila folders, documents in his neat chicken scratch, notes on difficult congregation members and how he could encourage them, finances, old journals, old materials for sermon prep. There were pictures of me, him, and my mother: at Disney, on Lake Michigan, at the fair, me with a white bow in my hair and lace socks poking out over my white dress shoes, us in our Sabbath best. With the Adventist apocalyptic idea of the world ending at any time, we had to be prepared for the unexpected, desired coming of Christ. Most things were a means to an end, with the hope of heaven being first in our heads. Relationships, elation, and desire were all fragments of what was to be expected in the next life, where we would be united with God. In his theology, my daddy believed that when you die you don't meet your maker. Instead you wait, laying in the cold hard ground until the trumpets of heaven call all of us home. His eyes were fixed on glory, while I wanted him to see me while he was in the flesh.

As I shuffled through the files, I imagined him beneath me, buried in dirt. I stomped my feet wondering if he heard me, felt me. Was he comfortable or cold and sober? Did he regret it? Was he losing hope of being raised up?

On my knees, I put files in banker's boxes. I placed books in laundry baskets, flipping through his Hebrew and Greek Bibles from seminary. I scurried through journals searching for a mention of myself, his penmanship too scraggly to understand. Useless, I stacked them in three-by-three rows, neatly in the corner of the office. I swept and mopped the floor, pulled the blinds and dusted them, and washed the windows. I wiped down the book cases.

With lemon Pledge and a duster, I worked to make his desk perfect. As a child it was off-limits; I'd never looked inside it. I took the paper towel and wrapped it around my fingernails, using pressure to get grout out of every crevice. I opened up the desk drawer and pulled out everything and threw it on top. Toward the back, in a manila folder, were more pictures, ones I had never seen: my mother, younger and topless, her tongue sticking out and her hands behind her back; Daddy hiking Charlies Bunion, his face tight, a small smile; a Christmas party with Miss Birdie in the middle, grinning under mistletoe and my parents, glassy-eyed on either side and kissing her cheeks; a picture of me as a baby in his father's arms. On the back he had written, *My Dad and My Majorie, Christmas 1983.* At the back of his drawer was one more photo: Miss Birdie sitting in my father's lap, his arm around her waist, hers looped around his neck. *My Girl,* it said at the bottom.

Out of breath, I laid on my back and felt the wave come back over me. At the funeral home, the director had given me a pamphlet about the five stages of grief, but they were out of order in my life; the second step where the fourth should be, the fifth out of sight.

Over the desk was the buck head, with its glassy eyes, peering down at me. It was dusty and untouched; neither my mother nor I had looked at it when he had first received the gift. He showed it off to every visitor and house guest that came through. Once, when a deacon from Tennessee came to visit, Daddy called it his "one prized possession."

This was years before the divorce. My mother excused

herself to the guest bathroom. As I walked to follow her I turned back to look at him, eating with his colleague, suspended in their time with such focus. Our tables were set there with mismatched china. I wanted to walk in and hurl them back in his face. My mother, in the bathroom, boo-hooed, mascara all down her face. She sat on the toilet and looked out the window, one leg crossed over her knee, her toenails were chipped. She held her fingers and tissue to her mouth. She threw her hands up. The whole time I was there, sitting on the bathroom floor, watching.

"Everybody else, every other thing, gets his full attention. He looks at that damn elk how I want him to look at me!"

When the furniture was moved out, one of the men from the mission told me I should hold on to the desk, that I could make bank on the antiques.

"Thanks, but I'm ready to let it go," I said.

"That's a Queen Anne–style desk. You could get thousands. It's not something to really let go of. Hold on to your money, you know?" He patted me on the back. I curled away from him.

He was sweating from moving all the furniture, his gray shirt was now almost black. He was one of those plain, forgettable-looking people, as if I only could see him like a child's drawing—his ears, nose, and head shape.

"Thanks, but I'm ready to let it go."

He was in disbelief, as if I was biggest dumb-dumb on the planet. His enamel name tag read *Sylvester*. He went to open his mouth.

"Let me stop you right there." I squinted and read his name again. "Sylvester, right?" if it matters that much to you, you can have it. And *you* can sell it!"

His face turned red as I turned my back to him and walked back to the kitchen. Miss Birdie was making fajitas. I could smell the white onion cracking in the olive oil, the garlic, and the lack of seasoning. I hated her.

After we ate, I called my mother to get away from Miss Birdie. Jax had an acupuncture appointment with a master teacher in Charlotte. She was loading the car with their luggage, making sure she hadn't forgotten anything. "That's just how Birdie is. She's lonely. She overgives, she means well, but it gets her in trouble. She gets off on being needed." Their lab, Sunshine, barked in the background, I heard the sound of the hatchback lifting.

"I would say just ask your father, but that would just be insensitive. But he could tell you all about her, trust me."

"Sounds like you could, too," I said under my breath.

"Mmmmm." She paused. "Sounds like this is a hard time, sweetie. I'm sure a lot is coming up for you. Be gentle with yourself."

My throat got tight and hot, my eyes watered.

"Well I better get going, mom. I've got a lot more to do here. It's a big house, you know."

"She's not perfect. But be grateful for Miss Birdie," she said. "I was so alone in that marriage, at least you have someone taking care of you."

During the days I thought of my father, about him and Birdie. In the evenings, I dreamed of my mother coming to get me, breaking in through my window, her hair long and wrapping around me until I was warm, us wandering through the sky, an ocean of me and her. I wanted to tell my mother about Miss Birdie, how it freaked me out how touchy and warm she was, how somehow I was still softening to her. She knew when I was hungry before I did, she asked if I needed water, asked if I wanted to process anything, was always there, ready to comfort me, to quickly ease the suffering. She held my hand like a leash. Once, on a bad night, she'd stayed with me into the early morning while my tears were endless. She sat at the foot of my bed, patting my thigh. "You just have to let it out," she told me. I woke to her sleeping beside me, our bodies face to face, my mouth breathing in her breath. Panicked, I got up and slept on the couch in the living room. She woke me up later in the morning to coffee and biscuits. "I wondered where you went," she said, sitting beside me, tucking the blanket around my legs. My chest burned. "You feeling okay, Marjorie?"

When I was eight my family moved to Collegedale in the summer, a hot sprawl of sweltering months with my days spent making myself seen, not heard. Our parsonage was sparse and airy. My room was in the attic. That summer was the last of the tent revivals, with Daddy pitching large five-by-twenty tents on the eve of his installation service. Out in the boonies, the rolling, gauzy linen spread in the night air, making shadows over the full grass.

Under the black of night, the week-long service was struck by anticipation of the spirit arriving. There had always been charlatans—those who caught prematurely, falling back, sometimes splitting the back of their skulls to the white meat. But sometimes when the Spirit was right, people would get slain and fall out. The magic of connection was palpable in those moments, delicious, and it seemed my father had the ability to bring the strength of God directly into our house of worship, no matter how shabby. *Where two or more are gathered, only grazed what we could do.* Under his leadership, I saw lives changed, hearts softened, plans redirected, and broken spirits made new.

Beneath the tents, I waited with excitement in the evenings. The nights were long and uncomfortable, with sweat pulling at my temples. My clothes itched and mosquitoes tore up my legs, and I made x's in the raised bumps. Other deacons called me sweet-blooded and licked their lips, their stomachs buckling out of their thin three-piece suits. Armpits gray with summer sweat, I was getting too big to sit on my mother's lap. "Marjorie," she whispered, chiding me, as I climbed up on to her, my eight-year-old torso already the length of hers at thirty-five. I made my limbs deadweight in the hopes she'd wrap her arms around me. Her back became stiffer, and she patted my back with her palm. I felt silly engulfing her: the stoic, pretty first lady, and me, her big, needy baby.

As we sat there and listened, I watched the words connect with the people who needed it most. Older deacons nodded in approval as my father walked through the book of Job. The power of dejection, he mentioned; how Job was scorned, lied to, deceived, yet still kept the audacity of faith. In between pauses he took sips of water out of a jade carafe and wiped his forehead down with a tawny rag.

When people felt the Spirit come through like a rip tide, no one could outswim it. An undoing; a trove of white doves released by a string. I saw people drop like flies as my own eyes bulged with tears; the heavy feeling of belonging overtook me. As the saints groveled on the floor, ushers brought blankets and suit cloth to cover the legs of women, too inebriated to understand their indecency. I saw a woman spread so wide, I could see the edges of her graying pubic hair poking out the side of her black high-cut French briefs. My mother never fell out, only sobbed lightly as if on command, and all I could feel was a bubbling that started in the front of my ribs and worked down my spine. This presence was otherworldly, like the god of the universe, who set the sun spinning, who kept my heart pumping, was among us, intimately interested, nowhere he'd rather be, and my father had brought him here.

Miss Birdie and I started fighting. A wall grew between us. She didn't think I was dealing with my pain well. I didn't trust her. I kept thinking of her picture in Daddy's drawer and what she was hiding from me. How much did she know? She was always prodding. "You should talk about it more, sweetheart. I know it's eating at you." My face would get hot. I was tired of her coddling me, nursing my every need. I didn't need a mother, I had one. I didn't want a lover. I was beside myself. I just wanted someone to see me, hold me. No talking. No one ever held me. But I wasn't six in the pews any more. I wasn't ten at a summer revival. This was my life now. Almost thirty, scared, godless, and alone. We were set to have another movie night. She came tapping at my door, she twisted the handle, but I'd locked it. "Marjorie, let me be here for you. I want to be here for you." After an hour, I opened the door, my eyes swollen. "Please, get your things and leave," I told her. "Thank you for everything. Now I need you to leave." She stood still. "Oh, how I love you, Marjorie. I know you don't mean this. It's just the sad talking."

She looked at me and nodded. My face was flat. She frowned and held my cheek. "I always wondered which one you were more like, who you'd turn out to be. Sometimes when I look at you, when I see you, all I see is him. You call me when you're ready."

Before she moved out, she left me all the casseroles in clear, Pyrex dishes. Veggie stroganoff was what I was craving, with white rice and pinto beans. I walked through the hallway to the kitchen in the pitch dark. I walked with my head straight forward, hoping someone would be lurking in a corner, put a pillowcase over my head, and drag me to an unmarked Suburban. I would go with ease.

At the kitchen table I took out the dish and spooned myself a whole plate full. Placing the plate in the microwave, I saw the orange light whir in the black of the kitchen. I sat in the dining room facing the land—all those trees Daddy planted and the river beneath them—and cried into the stroganoff. The food was getting wetter and wetter, soaking in myself. The moon, just past full, swallowed the night, weeping its orange rind glow onto the grass. The oaks and the cicadas sang their haunts.

I was watching the moon shine its silver light down on God's big earth, and for a second, my pain was cauterized. The animal inside me stirred. I was night-drooling, reveling in the quiet of the evening, when I saw something like a woman coming up out of the water. Like Pharaoh's daughter wading in those reeds, I was watching something ancient.

When she started walking toward the back porch, I felt a shiver down my spine. I walked backward, watching her come closer. I went to the drawer, grabbed a steak knife, and walked back to her. I stood still right there, awash in a light: braless, stuffed, slobber dried all down my face. The knife was at my side bearing on the cellulite in my thigh. And wouldn't you know, Miss Birdie stood right there in front of me, staring through the glass right back. She was covered in dirt, blood smeared all over her forehead. I closed my eyes, counted back from ten, and dropped the knife, convinced of my grief-induced insanity.

When I opened my eyes, I searched those panes up and down.

I was looking in the windows for somebody, for Daddy, for her.

It was only me. ✳

ACKNOWLEDGEMENTS

Thank you to Hub City Press for publishing this book, trusting these stories, and nurturing them—and me—as they developed and came into the world. I feel extraordinarily lucky to have worked with such an intentional group of individuals (Betsy Teter, Meg Reid, Kate McMullen, and Julie Jarema to name a few) who are changing the landscape of publishing and making space for voices traditionally excluded from the American South.

Thank you to my sharp, kind, and patient editor, Katherine Webb-Hehn, who understood the vision of *Good Women* from the beginning. You worked along-side me, day by day until we got it right. Your intuitive eye made the book better.

Thank you to my mother, Nedra Hill, and my brother, Hallerin Hill II, for your irreplaceable companionship, presence, humor, patience, and support over these past six years. I love you both dearly and I am so grateful you are my family.

Thank you to C. Rizleris for your care and encouragement.

Thank you to the MFA Writing program at Savannah College of Art and Design, particularly to Dr. Nicol Augusté, Dr. Vanessa Garcia, and my thesis advisor and chair, Professor Jonathan Rabb, who taught me the value of precision, research, and intention in fiction. Your support and mentorship shaped the foundations of this book.

Thank you to my creative writing mentor, professor, and friend, Christina Seymour, for pulling me aside after English class and telling me I was a writer almost ten years ago. Your gentle, consistent presence changed the course of my life.

Thank you to Mahrukh Agha, Kate Hornele, and Ashanti Pope, my MFA cohort peers turned family, who met me when I moved, completely terrified, to Savannah at twenty-two years old, and who walked and wrote alongside me through it all (remember when we survived the dreaded forty-five hour review?!).

Thank you to all my friends and writing partners who believed in these stories and believed I could tell them: Sara Deatherage, Gardner Dorton, Mik Grantham, Lauren Lauterhahn, and Sarah Walker.

And finally, thank you to my grandmother, Lillian Annette Jackson Bolden, and my great-grandmother, Luvella Juanita Wright Smith. You showed me the stories and the heart.

I will never forget you. I hope to make you proud.

The COLD MOUNTAIN *Fund*

S E R I E S

NATIONAL BOOK AWARD WINNER Charles Frazier generously supports publication of a series of Hub City Press books through the Cold Mountain Fund at the Community Foundation of Western North Carolina. The Cold Mountain Series spotlights works of fiction by new and extraordinary writers from the American South. Books published in this series have been reviewed in outlets like *Wall Street Journal, San Francisco Chronicle, Garden & Gun, Entertainment Weekly*, and *O, the Oprah Magazine*; included on Best Books lists from NPR, *Kirkus Reviews*, and the American Library Association; and have won or been nominated for awards like the Southern Book Prize, Crooks Corner Book Prize, and the Langum Prize for Historical Fiction.

The Say So • Julia Franks
George Masa's Wild Vision • Brent Martin
The Crocodile Bride • Ashleigh Bell Pedersen
You Want More: The Selected Stories of George Singleton
The Prettiest Star • Carter Sickels
Watershed • Mark Barr
The Magnetic Girl • Jessica Handler

HUB CITY PRESS gratefully acknowledges support from the National Endowment for the Arts, the Amazon Literary Partnership, and the South Carolina Arts Commission.